The

T

They thought the horrible deaths had ended.

They thought the hot water could no longer scald them.

The spirit that had controlled both Jennifer Daly and Kimmy Bass had been battled by cheerleader Corky Corcoran. And Corky had won.

But something's still not right at spring cheerleading camp. The strange occurrences and terrifying accidents can mean only one thing . . .

THE EVIL SPIRIT NEVER LEFT!

But where is it now?

Books by R. L. Stine

Fear Street: THE NEW GIRL
Fear Street: THE SURPRISE PARTY
Fear Street: THE OVERNIGHT
Fear Street: MISSING
Fear Street: THE WRONG NUMBER
Fear Street: THE SLEEPWALKER
Fear Street: HAUNTED
Fear Street: HALLOWEEN PARTY
Fear Street: THE STEPSISTER
Fear Street: SKI WEEKEND
Fear Street: THE FIRE GAME
Fear Street: LIGHTS OUT
Fear Street: THE SECRET BEDROOM
Fear Street: THE KNIFE
Fear Street: PROM QUEEN
Fear Street: FIRST DATE

Fear Street Super Chiller: PARTY SUMMER
Fear Street Super Chiller: SILENT NIGHT
Fear Street Super Chiller: GOODNIGHT KISS

Fear Street CHEERLEADERS: THE FIRST EVIL
Fear Street CHEERLEADERS: THE SECOND EVIL
Fear Street CHEERLEADERS: THE THIRD EVIL

HOW I BROKE UP WITH ERNIE
PHONE CALLS
CURTAINS
BROKEN DATE

Available from ARCHWAY Paperbacks

FEAR STREET®
R·L·STINE

CHEERLEADERS
The Third Evil

WITHDRAWN

AN ARCHWAY PAPERBACK
Published by POCKET BOOKS

New York   London   Toronto   Sydney   Tokyo   Singapore

AN ARCHWAY PAPERBACK *Original*

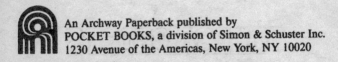

An Archway Paperback published by
POCKET BOOKS, a division of Simon & Schuster Inc.
1230 Avenue of the Americas, New York, NY 10020

Copyright © 1992 by Parachute Press, Inc.

ISBN: 0-671-75119-0

First Archway Paperback printing October 1992

10 9 8 7 6 5 4 3 2 1

FEAR STREET is a registered trademark of
Parachute Press, Inc.

AN ARCHWAY PAPERBACK and colophon are
registered trademarks of Simon & Schuster Inc.

Cover art by Edwin Herder

Printed in the U.S.A.

IL 7+

PART ONE

Team Spirit

Chapter 1

In the Soup

Miss Green's whistle echoed off the high ceiling of the gym. The cheerleaders stopped in midcheer as their advisor raised both hands to her head and pretended to tear out her frizzy brown hair. Her eyes were wide with exasperation.

Corky Corcoran sighed. That routine was going really well, she thought. Why did Miss Green stop us?

She cast a glance down the line of cheerleaders to her friend Kimmy Bass. Kimmy mopped her forehead with the sleeve of her T-shirt. She also appeared to be annoyed by the interruption.

It was warm for early April. The air in the gym felt hot and damp. Corky had her blond hair pulled straight back and tied in a high ponytail. She and the five other Shadyside High cheerleaders were dressed in Lycra shorts and loose-fitting T-shirts, which were drenched in perspiration from the after-school practice.

"Hannah, do me a favor," Miss Green said. "Step forward and show my *veteran* cheerleaders the proper way to do a round-off back tuck."

Hannah Miles bounced forward obediently, a broad smile on her pretty face. "I like to start in this position," she said, not at all embarrassed at being singled out. "You know—with my knees bent a little so I get more spring."

A slender, graceful freshman, Hannah was the only new member of the Shadyside High squad after spring tryouts. She replaced Megan Carman, who was graduating in June.

Hannah had long, straight black hair that she wore in a single thick braid to her waist and dark brown eyes that were constantly flashing with excitement.

She performed her back tuck, flipping high off the floor and landing perfectly on both feet. Then, without a pause, she performed a second back tuck just as stylish as the first.

"How was that?" she asked innocently, straightening her T-shirt.

"She thinks she's really great," Ronnie Mitchell whispered bitterly to Corky.

"She *is* great," Corky whispered back. Hannah's making us all look like clumsy elephants, Corky thought. She watched Hannah flash Kimmy a smile as she rejoined the line of girls.

Kimmy and Debra Kern were co-captains of the

4

squad, and Hannah had started playing up to them, asking for advice and fishing for compliments.

We all know Hannah is good. Why does she have to show off all the time? Corky wondered. Then she had to admit to herself: I guess I'm a little jealous.

At the beginning of the year Corky and her sister Bobbi had been the stars, the flashiest, most enthusiastic, and talented cheerleaders on the squad. But so much had happened since then.

So much horror . . .

Bobbi was dead. And so was Corky's boyfriend, Chip.

Both of them murdered by an ancient evil spirit. An evil spirit that had inhabited two of the cheerleaders. First Jennifer Daly. Poor Jennifer, also dead. Then Kimmy.

Corky had rescued Kimmy from the evil.

Afterward Corky thought she could push away the terrifying memories by throwing herself into her cheerleading. By making herself go on with her life.

But sometimes it was hard. Hard to forget. Hard to go on. And hard to be just one of the squad members.

I'm not even co-captain, Corky thought, glancing unhappily at Debra.

I'm a better cheerleader than Debra, she thought. Everyone knows it.

But before spring tryouts Miss Green had explained her decision to Corky. "Corky, I'm afraid you just don't need the pressure of being co-captain," she had said with genuine concern. "I mean, after . . . all that has happened."

All that has happened.

Corky shook her head, tossing her ponytail, trying to shake away her bitter thoughts.

Debra's my friend, she told herself. There's no point in being jealous of her.

"Corky—did you hear one word I said?" Miss Green's husky voice broke into Corky's thoughts.

"Yes. Of course," Corky lied, feeling her cheeks grow hot.

"Then let's try the football chant again," Miss Green said, staring hard at Corky.

Kimmy leapt forward, clapping her hands, and turned to the five other girls. "Okay. Ready? On three."

She counted to three, and they began their chant, their voices rising with each repetition, stomping and clapping in the rhythm they had practiced:

> *"Tigers, let's score!*
> *Six points and more!* (stomp stomp)
> *Tigers, let's score!*
> *Six points and more!"* (stomp stomp)

"Louder!" Kimmy urged, cupping one ear with her hand. "I can't hear you!"

> *"Tigers, let's score*
> *Six points and more!"*

"Still can't hear you!" Kimmy shouted.

As they repeated the chant even louder, Corky

glanced down the line to Hannah. Shouting enthusiastically, her hands in a high *V*, Hannah ended her chant and then spontaneously leapt into a tuck jump, rising high off the floor and slapping her knees at the peak of the jump.

What a show-off! Corky thought. Hannah knows we don't do a tuck jump here. Miss Green is going to get on her case now.

Corky turned her eyes expectantly to Miss Green. But instead of seeing anger on the coach's face, Corky was surprised to see approval—even a smile.

"I like that, Hannah," Miss Green declared. "That's a very clever finish." She turned to Kimmy. "What do you say? Let's try it again, and everybody do a tuck jump at the end."

"I don't believe it," Ronnie muttered to Corky, shaking her head.

"I believe it," Corky replied dryly.

"Hannah the Wonder Cheerleader!" Ronnie said under her breath.

Corky laughed and looked down the row of girls. Heather Diehl was leaning close to Debra, whispering something in her ear. Kimmy flashed Corky a meaningful glance, then stepped forward, changing her expression of disapproval to a smile. She began the chant again.

"Tigers, let's score!
Six points and more!"

The girls repeated the chant, getting louder each time. Then they all ended with tuck jumps.

7

Corky watched Hannah out of the corner of her eye. Her tuck jump was the highest of all. Her dark eyes sparkled and her face radiated enthusiasm as she landed gracefully, clapping her hands. "That was *great!*" she exclaimed. "Can we do it again?"

"What's her problem anyway?" Kimmy asked, twirling her water glass between her hands.

"Her problem is she's terrific," Corky replied, squeezing against the wall as Debra slid beside her in the red vinyl booth. "And we're jealous."

"I'm not jealous of her," Ronnie said quickly. A thoughtful look creased her face. "Well, maybe just her hair." Ronnie had tight copper-colored curls, a tiny stub of a nose, and a face full of freckles. She was in ninth grade, but looked about twelve. "Hannah has awesome hair."

"She's stuck up," Kimmy offered. "She's so stuck up, she probably knows we're talking about her right now."

The four girls laughed. Practice had ended at four-thirty and they had driven to The Corner, a new coffeeshop a few blocks from school that had quickly become a hangout for Shadyside students.

"Hannah isn't so bad," Debra remarked, her eyes lowered to the menu. "She's just enthusiastic."

The other three stared at Debra in surprise.

"Since when are *you* her best friend?" Kimmy asked sarcastically.

Debra raised her icy blue eyes from the menu. "I'm not. I just said she isn't so bad. She isn't mean or anything." Debra had straight blond hair cut very short. She was thin, almost too thin, and seldom smiled, an unlikely combination for a cheerleader.

"So we have one vote for Hannah," Kimmy said, making a one in the air with her index finger. "Anyone else?"

Before Corky or Ronnie could cast a vote, the waitress interrupted to take their orders. Kimmy and Ronnie ordered hamburgers and Cokes. Debra ordered a plate of french fries and a chocolate shake. No matter what she ate, she never put on weight.

When Corky ordered a bowl of split pea soup, the others erupted in disapproval. "Yuck!" Ronnie exclaimed, sticking a finger down her throat. "I may *hurl!*"

"I happen to *like* pea soup," Corky insisted.

"You're weird," Kimmy told her. "You're definitely weird."

"Is Hannah going out with anyone?" Corky asked, deliberately changing the subject.

"You ever see the guys hanging around her locker after school everyday?" Ronnie asked. "It's disgusting. Their tongues hanging out of their mouths. They practically drool on her!"

"Tsk-tsk." Debra clicked her tongue. "Sounds to me like you're jealous, Ronnie."

Ronnie stuck her tongue out at Debra. "So?"

"I think she's going out with Gary Brandt," Kimmy offered. "At least, I saw them together at the mall Saturday night."

"Gary's kinda cool," Ronnie said, fiddling with her silverware.

"Kinda!" Debra agreed with unusual enthusiasm.

"Hey, can you picture Hannah making out with Gary?" Ronnie asked, grinning. She performed a cheer: "Go, Gary, go! Go, Gary, go! Yaaaay!"

Everyone laughed.

"Know what?" Kimmy added. "Every time he kisses her, she probably does a tuck jump!"

More laughter.

"Hey, are you guys ready for next week?" Corky asked, changing the subject again.

"I'm already packed," Ronnie said. "I can't wait. This'll be the best spring break ever!"

"A whole week away from home," Corky said, sighing. "A whole week away from my pesty little brother."

"Maybe we'll meet some guys," Ronnie said, grinning. "You know, college dudes."

"You guys are in for a shock," Debra said dryly. "There'll be no time to hang out and meet guys. Cheerleader camp is *torture*. You work your buns off exercising in the morning, practicing new cheers all afternoon, going to workshop after workshop. Then at night you kill yourself competing against the other squads."

"Bobbi and I went to a cheerleader camp one summer in Missouri before we moved here," Corky recalled. "We worked hard. But we also did some partying."

"The Madison College campus is supposed to be pretty," Ronnie said. "My cousin told me the dorm we're staying in is brand new."

"Maybe we'll all room together!" Ronnie exclaimed. "It's going to be awesome!"

10

Everyone agreed except for Debra. "It's hard work and a lot of pressure," she warned. "You have to be enthusiastic and have a smile plastered on your face all day long."

When Ronnie and Debra got up to go to the rest room, Kimmy slid in beside Corky, a troubled expression on her face. "How are you doing?" she asked quietly.

"Okay, I guess." Corky shrugged.

"No. I mean *really,*" Kimmy insisted, her dark eyes staring into Corky's, as if searching for something.

"I'm doing a little better," Corky replied, fiddling with her silverware. "I don't think about things as much. I force myself not to think about Bobbi or Chip or—"

"I *can't* stop thinking about it," Kimmy said emotionally, clasping her hands tightly together on the Formica tabletop. "I keep thinking, what if the evil spirit is still around? What if it's still *inside* me?" Her voice cracked as she said this. She swallowed hard.

"Kimmy—" Corky started, resting a hand on Kimmy's arm. "I saw the evil spirit pour out of you. I saw it go down my bathtub drain. It's gone. You're okay now. You don't have to worry—"

"But how do we know it's gone for good? Corky, you got that note. The one that said it can't be drowned. And, Corky, sometimes—sometimes I feel so strange," Kimmy whispered, her eyes watering. She gripped Corky's arm and held it tightly. "Sometimes I—I just don't feel right."

The door to the coffeeshop opened and some guys from the basketball team walked in. One of them,

11

John Mirren, a lanky boy with short brown hair and a goofy grin, waved to Kimmy before sliding into a booth with his pals.

"Kimmy, we just have to pray that the evil spirit is gone for good," Corky said.

"But what if it isn't?" Kimmy demanded again.

Corky shrugged and felt a sudden chill. "It's *got* to be gone," she said, lowering her voice to a whisper. "I can't take any more death. I can't . . ." Her voice trailed off.

Debra and Ronnie returned, giggling and pushing each other playfully. They stopped when they saw the grim expressions on Corky's and Kimmy's faces.

"Hey—what's wrong?" Debra demanded. "You two still talking about Hannah Miles? Give the poor kid a break." She slid in across from Corky and Kimmy. Ronnie lowered herself into the booth beside Debra.

Corky forced a smile. "No, we weren't talking about Hannah."

"Do you know what other schools are going to be at the cheerleader camp?" Ronnie asked Kimmy.

Kimmy shook her head, tossing her crimped black hair. "I think there's going to be a squad from Waynesbridge. And maybe the cheerleaders from Belvedere."

"The ones that do all that rap stuff?" Ronnie asked.

"Wow, they're excellent!" Corky exclaimed. "Who else?"

"I don't know," Kimmy replied. "About a hundred cheerleaders total, I think."

The waitress appeared, carrying their orders on a

12

metal tray. "Who gets the pea soup?" she asked, staring at each girl.

Making disgusted faces, all three of her companions pointed to Corky. "Give me a break," Corky muttered. "I had a craving for pea soup. What's the big deal?"

The waitress set the food down and left.

"John Mirren waved at you," Debra said to Kimmy, squeezing the ketchup dispenser over her french fries. "I saw him as I was leaving the ladies' room.

"So?" Kimmy asked defensively.

"So maybe he likes you," Debra said. She put down the ketchup and reached for the salt.

Kimmy shrugged.

"He's a funny guy," Ronnie said, around a mouthful of hamburger. "He's a riot in science lab. Were you there last week when he spilled the hydrochloric acid?"

"That sounds hilarious," Debra said sarcastically.

"You had to be there," Ronnie replied. The tomato slid out of her hamburger. She struggled to push it back in.

Suddenly Corky uttered a loud gasp.

The others looked up from their food. "Corky— what's wrong?" Kimmy cried.

Corky's eyes were wide with surprise. "Look—" She pointed down at her soup bowl.

The other three turned their eyes to the bowl. The thick green soup appeared to be bubbling.

"Why is it doing that?" Ronnie asked, leaning forward to get a better look. "Oh!" she cried out, and pulled her head back as a gob of soup spurted up from the bowl.

"Hey—!" Corky cried in alarm.

The thick soup was tossing in the bowl, rising up against the edges like green ocean waves, bubbling higher and higher.

"Gross!"

"Yuck! It's alive!"

"What's going on?"

Like a green volcano, the soup rose up and spurted high in a thick, bubbling wave. Hot and steamy, more and more of it made a green tidal wave that began to ooze over the table.

"Hey—!"

"Help!"

"Get up, Kimmy! Let's *go!*"

The four girls scrambled from the booth as the steaming green liquid rose like a fountain, to plop onto the table and then ooze quickly onto the floor.

"What's that?"

"What's happening?"

"Where are they going?"

Voices rang out through the small restaurant. Confused kids gaped as Corky and her friends lurched down the narrow aisle, pushed open the front door, and fled to the sidewalk.

"The evil—" Corky managed to say, breathing hard, her heart thudding in her chest.

It's back, she thought.

The evil spirit is back.

Their anguished faces revealed that all four girls realized it.

The ancient evil spirit was back. It had been right at their table.

Was it inhabiting one of them? Possessing one of them?

Corky stared from face to face.

Which one? she wondered. Which one?

Chapter 2

A Corpse

Corky glanced out at the crooked rows of gray stones in the Fear Street cemetery. "I still miss her," she told Kimmy, her voice breaking with emotion. "I still think about Bobbi all the time."

Kimmy shivered despite the heat of the late afternoon. She shielded her eyes against the lowering sun with one hand, her gaze following Corky's up the sloping hill of the old cemetery.

Debra and Ronnie had driven straight home, eager to get away from the restaurant, eager to get away from the evil that had erupted in front of them.

Kimmy had driven Corky home, to her house on Fear Street, but when they'd gotten there, neither wanted to be alone. They went out for a walk and ended up just a block beyond the house at the cemetery.

The cemetery where Corky's sister, Bobbi, was buried.

Where Corky's boyfriend Chip was buried.

Both victims of the evil. The ancient evil that was still alive and refused to die.

"Come on," Kimmy urged, tugging on the sleeve of Corky's T-shirt.

With a sigh Corky turned away from the cemetery and began walking slowly back along the narrow, cracked sidewalk toward her house. "That was so *disgusting!*" she exclaimed, shaking her head. "All that hot green slime bubbling over everything. I'll *never* eat pea soup again!"

Shadows from the old trees overhead danced on them as they made their way slowly past the graveyard. The air suddenly grew cooler.

"The spirit was warning us," Kimmy said softly, "telling us that it's still here." She stopped beside her car and uttered a loud sob. "Oh, Corky—what if it's still inside *me?*"

Corky turned quickly, her features tight with fear, and hugged her friend. "It can't be," she whispered soothingly. "It can't be. It can't be."

"But how do I *know?*" Kimmy asked, and pulled away from Corky. Her round cheeks were pink and glistening with tears. Her crimped black hair was in disarray. Her dark eyes, locked on Corky, revealed her terror.

"I watched it leave you," Corky said, trying to calm her friend. "I watched it pour out."

"I don't remember any of it," Kimmy admitted. "All of those weeks. That whole part of my life. I don't remember a thing. It's as if I wasn't there."

"But now you're *you* again," Corky insisted. "Now you feel like *you,* right?"

Shadows washed over Kimmy's face. Her expression grew thoughtful. "I—I guess," she replied uncertainly. "Sometimes I don't know. Sometimes I feel crazy. Like I want to scream. Like I want to throw myself on my bed and just cry."

"But you don't, do you?" Corky demanded.

"No, I don't." She grabbed Corky's arm. Her hand, Corky felt, was ice cold. "Corky—what if it wants to kill someone else? What if it wants to kill us all?"

"No!" Corky cried with emotion. "No! We'll find it. We'll stop it. Somehow we'll stop it, Kimmy."

Kimmy nodded but didn't reply.

Corky stared hard at her. She wanted to reassure Kimmy. She wanted to convince Kimmy that the evil spirit no longer possessed her.

As Corky studied her friend's face through the thickening shadows, doubts began to gnaw at her mind.

Would Kimmy know if the evil spirit was still inside her?

If she did know, would she *admit* it?

As Corky stared at her, Kimmy's face began to glow. Her blue eyes lit up as if from some inner light.

Corky shut her eyes.

When she opened them, her friend appeared to be normal again.

"Call you later," Corky said, and took off on a run up to her house.

* * *

18

"Hi, I'm home!"

Corky closed the front door behind her and stepped into the living room. "Anyone home?"

No reply.

The house smelled good. Corky inhaled deeply. She recognized the aroma of a roasting chicken from the kitchen.

Home, sweet home, she thought, feeling a little cheered.

She turned toward the stairway. A pile of neatly folded clothing lay on the bottom step. Laundry day. Corky stooped to pick up the bundle, then made her way up the stairs to deposit it in her room.

Cradling the freshly laundered clothes in both arms, she stepped into her bedroom. Her eyes went to the windows, where the white curtains were fluttering. Then to the bed.

"No!"

The clothing fell from her arms as she began screaming.

Lying in her bed, tucked under the covers, was the hideous, bloated head of a corpse.

Chapter 3

Night Visitors

Corky stood gaping in horror at the lifeless, distorted face. She didn't see the closet door swing open.

"April Fool!" Her little brother Sean leapt out and began laughing uproariously.

"Sean!"

He slapped his knees, then dropped to the floor and began rolling on the carpet, uttering high-pitched, hysterical peals of laughter. "April Fool! April Fool!"

"Sean—you're *not* funny!" Corky cried angrily. She swung her arm, playfully trying to slug him, but he rolled out of her reach, still laughing.

"Stop it!" Corky snapped. "Really, Sean! You're not funny. You're just *dumb.*"

Stepping over the clothing she'd dropped, Corky strode over to the bed.

How could I have fallen for this? she asked herself.

The stupid head doesn't even look real. It's all green and lumpy. And it has only one ear!

"Gotcha!" Sean taunted, getting the most from his victory.

"I only pretended to be scared," Corky told him, turning away from the bed.

"Yeah. Sure," he exclaimed sarcastically. "I gotcha, Corky!" He climbed to his feet, ran to the bed, and grabbed up the head in two hands. "Think fast!" He heaved it at her.

Corky stumbled backward but caught it.

"Cool, huh?" Sean asked, grinning. "I made it myself. Out of papier-mâché. In art class."

Corky turned it in her hands, examining it, a frown on her face. "What kind of grade did you get for this mess?" she demanded. "An F?"

"We don't get grades in art, stupid!" Sean replied.

"Don't call me names," Corky snapped.

"I didn't. I just said you were stupid."

She tossed the disgusting head back to him. "Watch out. I'm going to pay you back," she warned playfully. "It's my turn next."

"Oooh, I'm scared. I'm soooo scared!" he said sarcastically.

She hurried over to him, and before he could escape, reached up with both hands and messed up his blond hair. He punched her hard in the shoulder.

Then they went down to dinner.

That night, with a full moon casting a wash of shimmering, pale blue light into the room, Bobbi floated through Corky's bedroom window.

21

Corky watched her sister hover over her bed, her long blond hair glowing in the pale light, floating around and above her in slow motion as if underwater.

I'm dreaming, Corky thought.

But Bobbi seemed so real.

So alive.

Bobbi's blue eyes opened wide. She stared down at Corky, her arms undulating slowly as if she were treading water.

She wore a long, loose-fitting gown, like a nightgown, sheer and shimmering in the pale light filtering through the open window.

"Bobbi—what are you doing here?" Corky asked in the dream.

Bobbi's dark lips moved, but no sound came out.

"Bobbi, why do you look so sad?" Corky asked.

Again Bobbi's dark lips moved, dark blue lips reflecting the cold, cold moonlight. Her hair billowed slowly around her head.

Corky sat straight up and reached out toward her sister. But Bobbi floated just out of reach.

"I—I can't touch you," Corky cried, her voice breaking with emotion. She leaned forward, stretching, reaching as high as she could.

Still Bobbi floated inches away.

The blue light swirled around them now, becoming a whirlwind, silent and cold.

"Bobbi—what do you want?" Corky demanded. "Tell me—*please!*"

Bobbi, her lips moving, locked her cold blue eyes on Corky. She seemed intent on telling Corky something.

But Corky couldn't hear her, couldn't read her lips, couldn't understand.

"Why are you here?" Corky pleaded. "What are you trying to tell me?"

Bobbi floated lower toward her sister. The blue light continued to swirl around them, closing them in, shutting out the rest of the room.

"You look so sad, Bobbi. So sad," Corky said, feeling her breath catch, ready to cry. "Tell me. Please. Tell me why you're here."

Without warning, without displaying any emotion, Bobbi reached up and grabbed her own hair. She tugged hard. The hair lifted up, removing the top of Bobbi's head with it.

"Oh—*no*—*!*" Corky shrieked in surprise.

Bobbi remained silent, holding the top of her head by the hair, gesturing with her other hand.

"Bobbi, what are you *doing?*" Corky cried, frozen in place, too horrified to watch, too curious to turn away.

Bobbi bent down and floated even closer.

Closer.

Corky peered up into her sister's open skull.

"What is it, Bobbi? What are you showing me?"

Corky stared inside Bobbi's head. And gasped.

In the darkness the inside of Bobbi's skull appeared to pulsate and throb. But Corky's eyes adjusted quickly to the pale light, and she saw what was moving in there.

Thousands of squirming, crawling cockroaches.

Packed into Bobbi's head like coffee in a can. Their slender legs scrabbled over each other as their bodies bumped and slid in a horrifying silent dance.

"Ohhh."

Corky woke up, choking.

She struggled to catch her breath.

"Bobbi—?"

Her sister had vanished.

The blue light was gone, replaced by ordinary white moonlight.

Her nightshirt, Corky realized, was drenched with sweat. Her whole body trembled, chilled and hot at the same time.

"What's going on?" she wondered aloud, blinking hard, trying to clear her head. "I haven't dreamed about Bobbi in weeks and weeks."

She waited for the trembling to stop. Then, deciding to get a glass of water, she lowered her feet to the floor.

And stepped on something warm. Something crackly. Something moving.

"Oh!"

Corky jumped.

Something crunched under her foot.

Something crawled over her toes.

She stared down.

"No! Oh, no!"

Cockroaches.

Thousands of silent cockroaches, scuttling over the floor, over one another. Climbing over her feet. Starting up her legs.

Their bodies glistened dark blue in the moonlight as they swam silently over the floor. An undulating, bobbing, throbbing carpet of cockroaches.

24

Chapter 4

Burned

"Help me!"

Kicking furiously, trying to force the prickly cockroaches off her feet, Corky stumbled to her door.

"Mom! Dad! *Please!*"

With each step she could feel the cockroaches crackle and squash beneath her bare feet. Nausea swept over her.

"Help me!"

Bending to brush the glistening insects off her legs, she burst out of her room into the dark coolness of the narrow hallway.

"Mom! Dad!"

"Hey—what's going on?" Mr. Corcoran appeared down the hall in his bedroom doorway, wearing only pajama bottoms, rubbing his eyes, looking like a bear coming out of hibernation.

"Dad—!"

"Corky, what's the big idea?" He stepped into the hall, stretching his arms above his head with a loud groan.

"Cockroaches!" Corky managed to blurt out, still feeling sick, still feeling the prickly legs crawling up her legs.

"Huh?"

"Cockroaches!"

"Corky, I hope you didn't wake me up because there's a cockroach in your room," he warned. "This is an old house, and old houses sometimes—"

"What's all the racket?" Mrs. Corcoran interrupted, appearing suddenly behind her husband, brushing her blond hair back off her forehead. "Corky, what on earth—?" She ran to Corky and threw her arms around her. "You're shaking all over. What *is* it, dear?"

Corky tried to answer, but her voice caught in her throat.

She pulled away from her mother and grabbed her hand. Then she tugged her toward her bedroom.

"Cockroaches, Mom," she finally managed to say.

Her father followed, shaking his head. "That's all she keeps saying. 'Cockroaches.'"

They followed Corky to her room. "Look," Corky said. She stepped into the doorway and clicked on the ceiling light. She took a deep breath, trying to hold down the waves of nausea, and pointed to the floor. "Just look."

All three of them peered down at the wine-colored bedroom carpet.

"I don't see anything," Mr. Corcoran said quietly.

Mrs. Corcoran stared hard at Corky, concern troubling her face.

The cockroaches were gone.

"Hey, you guys woke me up!" Sean's angry voice echoed in the hallway.

They turned to see his blond head poke into Corky's room.

"Sean—did you play some kind of practical joke on your sister?" Mr. Corcoran demanded sternly.

Sean's face filled with genuine innocence. "Who —me?"

"Wow! We're here!" Corky exclaimed, staring out the bus window as it bumped through the small campus of Madison College, where the cheerleader camp was being held. The ride from Shadyside had been nearly an hour, and the girls had laughed and joked and sung the whole way.

"It's perfect!" Hannah declared excitedly. "All the brick buildings covered with ivy. Like a movie set!"

"But where *is* everyone?" Debra asked, leaning over Corky to see out the window.

"Spring break," Kimmy told her from the front seat.

"You mean—*no guys!*" Ronnie cried.

She looked so devastated, everyone laughed.

Simmons, the young blond bus driver, pointed out the large, domed gymnasium, then drove to a tall brick dormitory about a block from it. As the bus pulled to a stop, a young woman, a cheerleader camp employee, hurried out to greet the girls and give them their room numbers.

27

A few minutes later Corky, Kimmy, and Debra found themselves in their assigned room.

A large picture window overlooked the campus. The walls were lime green, the low ceiling bright yellow. Two small desks were pushed back to back in the middle of the room. A third desk stood against one wall between two low dressers. Over one of the dressers, someone had tacked up a poster of U-2.

"I claim this bed," Debra declared, tossing her backpack onto the narrow bed in front of the window. "I have to have a window."

Corky spotted the bunk bed on the opposite wall. "Do you want the top or bottom?" she asked Kimmy.

Kimmy shrugged. "Top, I guess."

"The campus is so much bigger than I thought," Debra said, staring out the window at the green quadrangle, a grassy square surrounded by brick classroom buildings and other dorms. "What a shame there's no one here."

"Just cheerleaders," Kimmy said. "Dozens and dozens of cheerleaders." She opened her suitcase and began to unpack, unfolding tops and sweat suits and balled-up socks, and jamming them into the top drawer of the low maple dresser beside the bunk bed.

Corky laughed and pointed. "You sure you brought enough socks?"

Kimmy's cheeks turned pink. She brushed a strand of hair off her forehead. "My feet sweat a lot." She glanced up at Corky. "Some of us don't like to wear the same socks for a month!" she teased. She pulled a worn brown teddy bear from the suitcase and tossed it up on the top bunk.

"Oh, wow," Debra exclaimed from across the room. "Kimmy, don't tell me you still sleep with your teddy bear!"

"Even my little brother gave up his teddy bear," Corky teased. "But your bear is really cute!"

Kimmy's cheeks burned even redder. "I don't need it to sleep with. I just . . . take it places. It's sort of a good-luck thing."

"I guess we can use some good luck," Debra said wistfully.

Her comment brought a chill to the room.

Everyone became silent. Debra, her arms crossed over her chest, continued to stare out the window, her suitcase still unopened.

Corky knew they were all thinking about the evil spirit. Had it followed them to camp? Was it in the room with them now, hiding inside one of them?

Without realizing it, Corky stared hard at Kimmy. Kimmy seemed so nervous. She'd been so tense on the bus that brought them from Shadyside that she hadn't joined in on the songs or any of the kidding around.

Sitting next to Debra in the back of the small bus, Corky had confided her dream. She told Debra about Bobbi pulling off the top of her head, about the cockroaches inside and the cockroaches she thought she saw on her bedroom floor.

She knew that Debra wouldn't laugh at her. Ever since the evil spirit had been revealed the previous fall, Debra had become obsessed with the occult, with ancient superstitions and spirits. She had begun wearing a crystal on a pendant around her neck, a crystal that she believed had special powers. And she read book after book on spiritualism, the occult, and the dark arts.

"I've been studying dreams," Debra had replied seriously, her icy blue eyes staring into Corky's.

"What could that awful dream mean?" Corky demanded. "I mean, it was just so *gross.*"

"Bobbi was trying to tell you something," Debra replied in a low voice. "She was trying to show you something."

"Show me what? Cockroaches?" Corky asked. "Why would she want to show me cockroaches?"

Debra chewed thoughtfully on her lower lip. She shook her head. "I don't know, Corky. I don't get it."

Corky wanted to forget the dream and enjoy the cheerleading camp. But the dream was hard to shake. It had followed her to the campus.

Had the evil spirit followed her too?

All three girls were shaken from their somber thoughts by a loud knock on their door.

Debra reached the door first and pulled it open. "Hannah! Hi!" she exclaimed.

Wearing a green T-shirt over black leggings, Hannah marched past Debra into the center of the room. She was lugging two large leather suitcases, one in each hand. She plopped them down and sighed. "Ugh."

"What's going on?" Debra demanded, closing the door and following Hannah back to the center of the room. Kimmy and Corky both stared at Hannah curiously.

"Can I room with you guys?" Hannah asked, reaching back to adjust her long braid behind her shoulders.

"Huh?" Corky cried in surprise.

"There's no room for me with Ronnie and Heather," Hannah declared. "They both filled up the dressers before I could start to unpack. And look at all the stuff I brought." She gestured to the two bulging suitcases.

"Your room is bigger," Hannah continued, gazing around. "There's nowhere for me to put my stuff in the other room."

"But, Hannah—" Kimmy started to object.

"And get this," Hannah said, ignoring Kimmy. "Ronnie took the top bunk even though I told her I can't sleep on the bottom. I mean, it just creeps me out to have someone sleeping above me. You know? But she was so stubborn—she refused to move down."

"What about the other bed?" Kimmy suggested. "There's a third bed, right?"

"Yeah. Sure," Hannah replied heatedly. "But Heather claimed it. She says she has to be by the window or else she can't breathe."

"I can understand that," Debra said, glancing at the bed she had staked out by the window.

"So can I room with you guys?" Hannah asked.

"But there are only three beds," Corky protested.

"Yeah. These rooms are designed for three," Kimmy added, gesturing around. "Three desks, three dressers, three beds."

Hannah sighed again and rolled her eyes unhappily,

her face drooping into a pout. "Well, would one of you trade with me?" she asked reluctantly.

"I'm all unpacked," Kimmy protested. She clicked her empty suitcase shut.

"Come on," Hannah urged in a tiny voice. "Somebody trade places with me. You've *got* to. I'm just too claustrophobic in the other room. I'll freak. I'll totally freak. Really."

She glanced from Debra to Corky, then back to Debra.

"Well . . . okay," Debra finally relented. "If it means that much to you, Hannah—"

"Yes, it does! Thanks, Debra!" Hannah cried. And to Debra's surprise, Hannah rushed over, threw her arms around Debra, and hugged her. "You're a real pal!" she squealed.

"No big deal," Debra said, casting an uncomfortable glance at Corky. She started to collect her things.

Hannah dragged her suitcases over to Debra's bed by the window.

"Hey, we're going to be late," Kimmy cried, glancing at her watch. "We're supposed to be in the gym at two o'clock."

"See you down there," Debra called. The door slammed behind her.

"Where's the gym?" Hannah asked, opening one of her suitcases and starting to unpack.

"It's that big gray building with the dome. Remember? We passed it on our way here," Corky told her.

"I'll never get unpacked in time," Hannah said. She turned to Kimmy. "Which dresser is mine?"

Kimmy pointed. "You've got to hurry. We get points taken off for being late."

"Even for practice? That isn't fair," Hannah protested. "Do we have to be in our uniforms?"

"Not for practice," Kimmy said. "Only at night for the competitions."

"We're going to win every night!" Hannah declared. "I just know it."

"That's the spirit," Corky said dryly.

"Corky, would you do me a big favor?" Hannah asked, unfolding a pair of jeans from the suitcase, the third pair she'd pulled out.

Why did she bring so many jeans? Corky wondered. Why did she bring two suitcases for a one-week stay?

"Sure. What?" she asked Hannah.

"Would you run me a hot bath?"

The request caught Corky by surprise. "What did you say?"

"Would you run a tub for me? I feel so grimy after that long bus ride. But I've got to get this stuff unpacked. And I don't want to be late. Please?"

Corky glanced at Kimmy. Kimmy made a funny face, crossing her eyes.

"Yeah, sure," Corky told Hannah. She started toward the bathroom in the corner.

"You're a pal," Hannah said, pulling two pairs of denim cutoffs from her suitcase.

I don't believe her nerve, Corky thought angrily. She really thinks she's a princess or something.

Corky pushed back the white plastic shower curtain, then bent down to turn on the water.

First Hannah complains that the other room is too small for her, Corky thought, getting even more annoyed. Then she orders me around like I'm a servant. It's really *unbelievable!*

She put her hand under the faucet to gauge the water temperature, then turned the knob to make it a little warmer.

"Okay, it's going," she told Hannah, returning to the main room.

"Thanks," Hannah muttered distractedly. She was arranging her makeup and other cosmetics on a dresser top.

"We'd better hurry," Corky said to Kimmy. She walked to the mirror and pulled a hairbrush back through her straight blond hair. "You ready?"

"In a sec," Kimmy replied. She disappeared into the bathroom, closing the door behind her.

"I guess we'll meet you in the gym," Corky told Hannah.

"Yeah, fine," Hannah said, starting to unpack her second suitcase.

Kimmy emerged from the bathroom. "Don't take too long," she warned Hannah.

Corky followed Kimmy out to the hallway. She closed the door behind her. She heard the latch click as Hannah locked the door from the inside. "Do you *believe* Hannah?" Corky asked as they started to walk toward the elevator.

Kimmy stopped short. "Oh, no! I forgot the pompoms. Miss Green said she was counting on me to remember them."

They both turned and made their way back to the room. "That was a close call," Kimmy said.

Kimmy reached for the doorknob.

But her hand stopped in midair as a scream rang out.

Both girls froze.

Another high-pitched shriek.

It was Hannah, Corky realized at once.

Hannah inside the room. Screaming in horror.

Chapter 5

"I Could Just Murder Her"

Corky fumbled in her bag for the room key. Kimmy pounded furiously on the door. "Hannah—what's wrong? Hannah!"

Her hand trembling, Corky finally jammed the key into the lock and pushed the door open.

As she and Kimmy hurtled into the room, Hannah came running out of the bathroom, a large maroon bath towel wrapped around her. Dripping water, she pointed an accusing finger at Corky, her eyes wide with anger.

"How *could* you?" she shrieked in a shrill, high-pitched voice. "How *could* you?"

"Hannah—what happened?" Corky demanded, gaping at her, bewildered.

"What happened?" Kimmy repeated right behind Corky.

"How *could* you? How *could* you?" Hannah repeated frantically. "You tried to *scald* me!"

"Huh?" Both Corky and Kimmy cried in unison.

"The water. It was so hot! I didn't know. I stepped right in. I trusted you."

"But, Hannah—" Corky started.

"Look at my legs!" Hannah screamed. "Look!" She lifted the towel to give the other two girls a better view. "You tried to *scald* me!" she repeated.

Corky lowered her eyes to Hannah's legs. Still dripping wet, both legs were bright red from the feet nearly up to the knees.

"But that's impossible. I *tested* the water," Corky protested.

Hannah glared furiously at Corky. "That's just so *mean!* I—I—I don't—" she sputtered.

"The water probably started coming in hotter after Corky left," Kimmy said, coming to Corky's defense.

"Really. I tested it. I did," Corky insisted, staring at the scarlet flesh of Hannah's legs.

Hannah pulled the towel around herself more tightly. She didn't reply.

"I wouldn't deliberately hurt you," Corky muttered.

"Should we get you to a nurse or something?" Kimmy asked.

Hannah shook her head. "They're starting to feel better. I was just shocked, that's all."

"I'm really sorry," Corky said, "but I know the water was okay when I left it."

Hannah shrugged. "Okay. Guess I overreacted."

"You sure you're okay?" Kimmy asked.

"Yeah. Fine," Hannah replied. She took a few steps

into the center of the room. "I guess I'm okay. Sorry I freaked like that." She turned and disappeared back into the bathroom.

"See you at the gym!" Kimmy called. "We'll explain to Miss Green why you're late."

Corky's mouth dropped open in a silent gasp as her sister suddenly flashed into her mind. Bobbi had died because of scalding-hot shower water, Corky remembered.

"I really did test the water," Corky muttered, more to herself than to Kimmy.

Kimmy picked up the carton of pom-poms. Then they headed out the door.

"Weird," Kimmy muttered, shaking her head as they walked quickly down the long corridor to the elevators. "Weird."

It sure is, Corky thought.

And then she remembered that Kimmy had gone into the bathroom while the water was still running.

That's right, Corky told herself. Just before we left the room, Kimmy went into the bathroom.

She glanced at Kimmy as the elevators came into view. Kimmy stared straight ahead, her face expressionless, revealing no emotion.

Did Kimmy go into the bathroom and turn the hot water up? Corky wondered.

Did Kimmy try to scald Hannah?

> *"Hey, America—the time is here!*
> *Shadyside, stand up and cheer!*
> *Here we come. We want the world to know*
> *Shadyside is the HIT OF THE SHOW!"*

Cheering loudly, the six Shadyside cheerleaders ended the routine with synchronized back handsprings.

"Ow!" Ronnie cried out, losing her balance and landing hard on her arm.

Miss Green blew her whistle as the other squad members clustered around Ronnie. Kimmy and Debra helped her to her feet.

"I'm okay," Ronnie insisted. "Really. I'm all right." She tested her shoulder, rotating her arm like an airplane propeller. "It feels okay."

"Then let's try the routine again," Miss Green said brusquely. She glanced at the sidelines, where one of the camp officials was scribbling notes rapidly on her clipboard.

Miss Green blew her whistle again.

Whistles were blowing all over the enormous gym. Cheerleading squads from fifteen different schools were shouting, dancing, leaping. Sneakers squeaked and thudded on the polished floor. Songs echoed off the tile walls.

What an amazing sound, Corky thought. I'll bet it doesn't sound like this anywhere else in the world!

A few feet away the cheerleaders of the Redwood Bulldogs were practicing rollups into partner pyramids. Their blue and gold uniforms, which they wore even though uniforms weren't required, looked fresh and new.

"Look at that girl. Their captain," Corky said to Kimmy, practically having to shout in her ear to be heard. She pointed to a cheerleader with beautiful long red hair. "She's really *awesome!*"

"I *know* her!" Kimmy exclaimed. "She used to go to my Sunday school. Her name is Blair O'Connell. She *is* awesome—and she knows it!"

They watched Blair perform an astounding cartwheel, then flip herself effortlessly up onto her partner's shoulders, her red hair flying like a victory pennant.

"Wow," Corky said, shaking her head in admiration. "She is really outstanding!"

"We can beat her!" Hannah cried, suddenly appearing behind Corky and Kimmy. "We'll just have to work harder, that's all! Come on, everybody!" Hannah shouted, clapping her hands. "Let's show the Bulldogs they're not so hot!"

Hannah acts as if *she's* the captain, Corky thought scornfully. But she found herself caught up by Hannah's enthusiasm anyway. Clearing her mind of all unpleasant thoughts, Corky threw herself wholeheartedly into the routine.

> *"Hey, America—the time is here!*
> *Shadyside, stand up and cheer!"*

As the Shadyside squad practiced its cheer, Corky saw Blair O'Connell watching, her arms crossed over her chest, a sour look on her face. As the routine ended and Ronnie again mistimed her backflip and fell, Corky saw Blair laugh gleefully as she pointed Ronnie out to one of the other Bulldog cheerleaders.

Kimmy stepped up beside Corky. She had obviously been watching Blair too. "I never liked her," she said in Corky's ear. "She's so stuck up, she's disgusting."

"But what a figure!" Corky exclaimed. "She's so tall and—and—look at that tiny waist and—"

Miss Green's angry voice interrupted their conversation. "We're not here as spectators," she scolded. "Let's start again. Ronnie, are you going to land on your feet or your butt this time?"

Ronnie blushed. Her upper lip glistened with perspiration. She tugged at her curly copper-colored hair and uttered a cry of exasperation. "I'll get it this time," she promised.

"Let's go! Let's go! Let's go!" Hannah cried, jumping up and down and clapping.

She's the cheerleader's cheerleader, Corky thought sarcastically. Her eyes went from Hannah to Blair. Two of a kind, Corky thought bitterly. Except that Blair is more talented.

Corky lined up with the others to begin the routine again. The gym grew hotter, the air thick and damp. The shouting voices, the cheers, the singing and clapping—it was all starting to make Corky's head spin. She closed her eyes for a brief moment, but the bright lights didn't fade. The echoing sounds only grew louder. She reopened her eyes and began the routine.

It went better. At least, Ronnie didn't fall. Again, Corky watched Blair O'Connell in her sleek blue and gold uniform, an expression of superior amusement on her beautiful face.

They did the routine one more time. Then Miss Green suggested they work on handsprings.

As they practiced, camp officials circulated and studied each team carefully, jotting down notes, having brief conversations with coaches and advisors.

Corky performed a handspring, then moved into a spread-eagle jump.

Pretty good, she thought, breathing hard. This is quite a workout, but I'm really getting into it.

She wiped the perspiration off her forehead with the back of her hand.

"Corky, can I give you a little advice?" Hannah said loudly, stepping up in front of her. It wasn't a question, Corky realized immediately. "You need to get more lift on your spread-eagle jump," Hannah instructed. "You're still a little too low."

"Huh?" Corky wasn't sure she was hearing correctly. Was Hannah, a freshman, really giving her advice in front of the entire squad?

"If you bring your feet in closer together, you can control your jump better," Hannah continued. "Watch. I'll show you."

She proceeded to perform a spread eagle, jumping high off the floor, her eyes on Corky the whole time, her long braid flying. She landed gracefully, a pleased smile on her face. "See?"

"Thanks, Hannah," Corky said without enthusiasm. "I'll try it." She turned quickly and walked over to Debra and Heather.

What unbelievable nerve, Corky thought angrily.

I don't mind taking advice from the other girls. But Hannah really thinks she's queen of the world!

She's only a freshman, after all. Bobbi and I were

all-state in Missouri. I think I can get along without advice from Hannah.

"Hey—lighten up!" Debra called, seeing Corky's angry, tight-lipped expression. "People are watching," she teased. "Ten points off if you lose your smile for a second."

Corky plastered a big, phony smile on her face for Debra's benefit.

"That's better," Debra said, laughing. She was fingering the crystal she always wore around her neck. She flashed Corky a thumbs-up sign, then returned to working on partner pyramids with Heather.

Corky hadn't noticed that Kimmy had come up behind her. She jumped, startled, when Kimmy started to talk. "Someone has to take Hannah down a peg or two," Kimmy said with surprising bitterness.

"Huh?" Corky hadn't realized that Kimmy had observed her jumping lesson from Hannah.

"She's the pits," Kimmy said through gritted teeth. "Sometimes I could just murder her—couldn't you?"

The way Kimmy said those words gave Corky a cold chill.

Sometimes I could just murder her.

Corky shrugged. "Hannah is Hannah, I guess."

Kimmy stared at her with no expression.

Whistles blew. The cheerleaders were being called to a meeting to hear about the evening competition. There would be minor competitions each evening. On the fifth and final night a major competition would be held. Each squad would perform its most complicated routine, and awards would be presented to the winners.

After the meeting Corky walked alone back across the quadrangle to the dorm. Her legs ached. She was hot and sweaty. What a workout! she thought.

Well, Debra had warned her that cheerleader camp was mostly hard work.

A cool late-afternoon breeze did refresh her as she made her way across the nearly deserted campus. A few college students circled the quadrangle on bikes.

She pulled open the glass doors to the dorm and stepped inside. Her sneakers squeaked on the marble floor as she crossed to the elevators. The lobby was deserted and quiet, but somewhere far down the hall, country music was playing.

Thinking about taking a long, cool shower, Corky stepped onto the elevator and rode up to the sixth floor. She stepped out and began walking along the dark carpet to her room.

To her surprise, her sneakers stuck to the carpet.

"What's happening?" she cried out loud, looking down.

The carpet appeared to be moving, undulating like waves.

"Hey!" Corky cried out.

She blinked. Once. Twice. Waited for her eyes to adjust to the dark hallway, to stop playing tricks on her.

She tried to walk, but the floor was sticky and wet. The carpet still moved in waves, thick and black, rolling over her sneakers.

"No!" Corky screamed. Can anyone hear me? she thought. Is anyone up here?

The entire carpet had become a dark, thick sea, rolling and tossing, swaying back and forth.

"I can't walk!" Corky screamed. "Is anyone here? Can anyone help me?"

Like bubbling tar, the thick liquid rose up and over her sneakers, over her ankles.

It's pulling me down, Corky realized.

I can't move.

It's so sticky.

It's pulling me down.

"Help!"

Chapter 6

First Cheers, Then Screams

"It's so sticky!" Corky cried again. "I—I can't move!"

She looked up to see Debra staring down at her, her normally calm features twisted in alarm.

"Corky—what *is* it? What are you *doing* down there?" Debra dropped to the floor and wrapped an arm around Corky's trembling shoulders.

"It's so sticky," Corky repeated, still dazed.

"Huh? What's sticky? What's happening?" Debra demanded frantically.

Corky realized she was on her knees. On the dark carpet.

The still carpet.

It was no longer rolling and tossing.

Confused, she rubbed the dry carpet with her palms. "Debra?"

Debra's eyes were locked on Corky. She kept her

46

arm protectively around Corky's shoulders. "Why are you down here, Corky? Did you fall?"

Corky raised herself back up on her knees. She shook her head. "No. I didn't fall. It pulled me down."

Debra's mouth dropped open. "Huh?"

"The carpet. It started to roll back and forth, then it turned into a sticky liquid. And tried to pull me down." Corky stared intently at Debra, trying to read Debra's expression, trying to see if Debra believed her.

Debra shut her eyes. "The evil spirit," she said, lowering her voice.

"Yes," Corky quickly agreed.

"It's here," Debra whispered. "I can feel it." Letting go of Corky, she moved her hand to the crystal that hung around her neck. With her eyes still closed, she twirled the crystal rapidly in one hand, then squeezed it tightly.

She opened her eyes and climbed to her feet, reaching down with both hands to Corky. "Here. Let me help you up," she said softly. "Let's get you back to your room."

"Who's doing this to me?" Corky asked, unsteadily resting one hand against the wall. "Who is *torturing* me?"

Debra shook her head, her expression tight-lipped and thoughtful. "I don't know, Corky," she replied, guiding Corky to her room. "I really don't know."

The Bulldogs won the evening competition easily. They performed an endless rap routine that wowed the judges. Blair O'Connell, with her beautiful red hair floating behind her, appeared to defy the laws of gravity with her jumps and flips.

The other cheerleaders, dozens of them, huddled with their squads, waiting to compete and gaping in obvious admiration as Blair confidently performed her flashy solo part of the routine.

"What a show-off," Kimmy whispered to Corky as Blair and the Bulldogs ended their rap routine with a series of synchronized flips. "Blair's not really graceful. She's just an acrobat."

Corky laughed. "The judges look impressed. Maybe they *like* acrobats."

Kimmy scowled and walked away.

"We can beat them! We're the best!" Hannah was shouting, clapping excitedly. "Tigers rule!" she cried.

The other girls picked up the rhythm, clapping with Hannah. "Tigers rule! Tigers rule!"

But when it came time for the Shadyside squad to perform, everyone was just a bit off. When both Ronnie and Heather mistimed their final tuck jumps, Corky realized that it wasn't their night. The Tiger cheerleaders trotted off clapping to join the audience to watch the next squad perform.

"We'll get 'em tomorrow night!" Hannah shouted enthusiastically. "We're psyched now! We're *psyched!*"

"Yeah! We'll get 'em!" Kimmy echoed, but she couldn't muster up the same enthusiasm as Hannah.

After Blair and the Bulldog squad received their first-place award, the red and-white-jacketed judge raised her hand for quiet. The roar of excited voices in the enormous gym became a hushed rumble.

"On the final night we will award a spirit stick to each member of the winning squad. The sticks will be painted with your school colors, and can be used to help inspire spirit at pep rallies," she announced, straining to be heard. "But on every other night we'll award a red spirit ribbon to the most spirited cheerleader on each squad. There's so much spirit in this gym tonight, it's *unbelievable!*" she cried, holding up the red ribbons in both hands. "I want you all to give yourselves a cheer and a round of applause!"

The gym practically shook from the exploding voices, stomping feet, and clapping hands.

When the cheering stopped, the judge called out the name of the red-ribbon winner on each squad. Blair O'Connell accepted hers casually with a broad smile and wave at her cheering teammates.

The winner on the Tigers was Hannah. She squealed with delight when her name was called, and drew a cry of surprise as she performed a cartwheel on her way to collect her prize.

Corky glanced at Kimmy, who rolled her eyes to the ceiling. Then Corky noticed that Debra was smiling broadly and clapping heartily for Hannah.

When Hannah came bounding back, holding the ribbon triumphantly over her head, Debra rushed forward and gave her a hug. The two girls walked off together, heading toward the exit.

Wow, Corky thought, following them with her eyes as everyone began filing out noisily. Since when is Debra such pals with Hannah?

Corky realized she was feeling a little jealous. Debra was *her* friend, after all.

"Corky—catch you later!" Corky looked up to see Kimmy calling to her, shouting over the excited voices of the crowd. Kimmy said something else, but the words were completely drowned out.

Corky slowly made her way through the crowd. As she passed Blair O'Connell, she overheard Blair boasting to another Bulldog cheerleader, a tall, pretty girl with a dramatically short hairdo. "Not much competition this year," Blair said snootily.

"It was better last year," her companion replied.

"Everyone's just so tacky," Blair complained.

She's deliberately talking loud so people will overhear her, Corky realized, frowning.

"Did you *believe* that nursery-rhyme routine?" Blair exclaimed, hooting and shaking her head. "What *is* this? Kindergarten or something?"

"There aren't even any cool guys around," the other cheerleader complained.

They drifted out of Corky's hearing.

They really are snobs, Corky thought. Especially Blair. She's good, but I've never seen anyone so stuck up.

I'd like to beat them one night, Corky told herself, feeling her anger rise. Just once. I'd like to show Blair O'Connell what real cheerleading is like.

Just once. I'd like to wipe that snobby, superior smirk off her perfectly perfect face.

Maybe tomorrow . . .

Later that night, tossing in her unfamiliar dorm-room bed, Corky again dreamed about Bobbi.

Bobbi floated in through the window, her long,

nearly transparent nightgown fluttering around her, her blond hair flying out around her face, circling her head in light.

"Bobbi!" Corky exclaimed in the dream.

As before, she reached out to her sister with both hands. And again felt the frustration, the heartbreaking frustration, of not being able to touch her.

"Bobbi, why are you here?"

Her dead sister hovered above Corky's bed, gazing down at her mournfully.

"Please, Bobbi—can't you tell me? Can't you tell me why you're here?"

Again Bobbi spoke, and again no sound came out of her mouth.

"Bobbi, you look so sad, so troubled. Tell me what's bringing you here," Corky pleaded.

Bobbi descended until she was just inches above the bed, staring down at Corky with mournful eyes.

And then, as in the previous dream, she grabbed her hair with both hands and tugged hard.

Her scalp pulled off, taking with it the top of her skull. Holding her scalp to one side, she leaned down so that Corky could see inside her head.

"No!" Corky didn't want to look. "Bobbi, please—don't make me—!"

She shut her eyes tightly, but couldn't keep them shut.

Corky couldn't help herself. She had to see what was inside.

Peering into Bobbi's open skull, she saw snakes, brown snakes, slithering over one another, hissing and rattling, snapping their venomous jaws.

Snakes rose up, lifting their slender triangular heads out over Bobbi's skull. Snakes poured down Bobbi's ears, slid down the back of her neck.

Hissing louder and louder, the snakes stared down menacingly at Corky with their flat black eyes.

Corky snapped awake in the heavy gray light of morning.

She bolted upright in bed, her heart pounding like a drum.

She heard hideous screams.

It's me. I'm screaming. Because of my dream, she thought.

I'm screaming and I can't stop.

Blinking hard to gaze through the dim light at the unfamiliar room, it took Corky several seconds to realize that she *wasn't* the one screaming.

The horrifying cries were coming from Hannah.

Chapter 7

A Bad Cut

"Hannah—what *is* it?"

Hannah's high-pitched shrieks continued.

Kimmy slid down from her top bunk just before Corky leapt out of her bunk. In the pale morning light washing in around the curtains, Corky could see Hannah sitting on her bed, her head bent forward.

As Corky moved closer, still half in her dream about Bobbi, almost expecting the floor to writhe with snakes, she saw that Hannah had both hands at the nape of her neck.

"Hannah! What's *wrong?*"

Hannah screamed again, staring at something on her lap.

"Are you dreaming?" Kimmy demanded.

"My hair!" Hannah screamed.

"Huh?"

53

"My hair! My hair! My hair!"

Corky reached up and turned on a bedside lamp.

She and Kimmy both cried out when they saw what was in Hannah's lap.

It was her braid.

"My hair! My hair! My hair!" Hannah shrieked, covering her face with her hands.

"But how——?" Corky started.

Kimmy stared down at the braid in open-mouthed horror. "It—it was cut!" she stammered.

Hannah sobbed loudly into her hands.

"But who *did* it?" Corky cried, staring at Kimmy. "You and I are the only ones who . . ." Her voice trailed off. She couldn't finish her sentence.

Suddenly Hannah grabbed the braid in one hand and thrust it up accusingly at Corky and Kimmy. "One of you did this to me," the girl said in a low, trembly voice. Tears ran down her cheeks as her entire body convulsed in an angry tremor.

She recovered quickly and jumped to her feet, holding the braid high, forcing Corky and Kimmy to step back. "Who?" she demanded, her horror giving way to fury. "Who? Who? Who?" she repeated, pushing the braid first in Corky's face, then in Kimmy's.

"No!" Corky cried. "I didn't. I *wouldn't!*"

"I didn't!" Kimmy also protested, glancing at Corky.

"Who?" Hannah repeated, sobbing. "Who? Who? It was one of you. It *had* to be. First the scalding bath. Now *this!*"

"We didn't do it," Corky cried. "You've got to

54

believe us, Hannah." She reached for Hannah's shoulders, intending to comfort her. But Hannah recoiled violently, her face twisted in anger.

"Why would we do such a horrible thing?" Kimmy asked. "Why?"

"Because you're jealous of me," Hannah snapped back. She held up the black braid. It looked like a small dead animal in her hand.

"Hannah—"

"You're both jealous of me," Hannah said, lowering her voice. She wiped the tears from her cheeks with her free hand. "You know I'm the best cheerleader at Shadyside. You know you can't compare."

"Hey, that's not fair!" Kimmy snapped. "We're all good."

Corky could see Kimmy's anger building, her muscles tightened, her hands balled into fists at her sides.

"You're new on the squad, Hannah," Kimmy said heatedly. Her cheeks were bright red, even in the morning light. Her chest heaved and she was breathing hard. "You don't know us very well. And I'm sorry to say it because I know you're really upset, but you don't know as much as you think you do."

Hannah's eyes flared. "I know *one* thing for sure," she said through gritted teeth, lowering her voice. "I know one thing. You want me out—you want me off the squad. So you think you can scare me—"

"That's not true!" Corky insisted shrilly.

"Well, I'm not quitting," Hannah declared, ignoring Kimmy and Corky. "No way. No way you're frightening *me* off the squad."

She stormed to the dresser and deposited the dark

braid carefully on the dresser top. "I'm staying on the squad even if I have to cheer bald!" Furiously, she pulled out the top drawer and began rummaging in it.

"Hannah—wait," Kimmy pleaded. "I didn't mean to lose my temper. What are you going to do?"

Hannah tossed a pair of denim cutoffs onto the bed and continued rummaging. "I'm going to get dressed," she answered, her voice tight. She glanced at her wristwatch, which lay beside the sad-looking braid on the dresser top. "It's almost breakfast time. I'm going to get dressed. Then I'm going to show Miss Green what you did to me."

"But, Hannah—" Corky started.

"Shut up!" Hannah screamed. "Both of you—just *shut up!*" She uttered another loud sob and pulled off the oversize T-shirt she'd been sleeping in.

Corky started to say something, but a sharp glance from Kimmy made her stop. Slowly Corky retreated to her bed and lay down on top of the tangled covers, with a loud sigh.

Her eyes followed Kimmy as she made her way across the room to the window and drew the curtain open. Her cheeks on fire, Kimmy pressed her face against the morning-cool glass and shut her eyes.

Corky shivered. She pulled the thin wool blanket up over her legs. She continued to stare at Kimmy, her mind spinning with unpleasant thoughts. Frightening thoughts.

It was obvious to Corky that Kimmy was the culprit.

Kimmy *had* to have been the one to cut off

Hannah's braid while she slept. No one else had been in the room.

That meant that Kimmy was also guilty of changing the bathwater, turning up the hot water so that Hannah would scald herself.

Kimmy had confided to Corky that she'd like to murder Hannah. And here she was, torturing Hannah.

The evil is here, Corky thought miserably. The evil is in this room. Still inside Kimmy. Poor Kimmy—she doesn't know.

It was all too horrifying, too horrifying to put into words. But words popped into Corky's mind:

Kimmy is not in control of her body. The ancient, evil force controls her now.

The door slammed shut then, jarring Corky from her thoughts. It was Hannah leaving the room.

Corky's eyes went to the dresser top. Hannah had taken the braid with her.

Kimmy turned away from the window, looking drained, lifeless. "Guess I'll get dressed too," she muttered.

"Kimmy—what are we going to do?" Corky demanded.

Kimmy shrugged and shook her head sadly. "Hey, Corky?" Her voice caught in her throat. She stared intently into Corky's eyes. "I'd remember if I cut off Hannah's braid, wouldn't I?"

It wasn't just a question. The words were too heavy with fear for it to be just a question.

She wanted Corky to reassure her, to tell her she was okay, she was normal. But Corky couldn't bring herself to lie to her distressed friend.

"I'd remember something like that, wouldn't I?" Kimmy repeated, sounding even more pitiful, more desperate.

"I don't know," Corky said softly, lowering her glance to the floor.

A short while later Kimmy, dressed for the morning exercise workout in Lycra shorts and a red tank top, headed out of the room. She stopped at the door and turned back to Corky. "You coming down to breakfast soon?"

"Be right there," Corky replied.

After Kimmy left, Corky stood up and stretched. Then she walked to her dresser, her mind spinning. She pictured Miss Green listening to Hannah's story. She imagined the shocked expression on the advisor's face.

Then what?

Will Kimmy and I be kicked off the squad?

Frowning, Corky pulled open her dresser drawer, started to reach for a clean T-shirt, and stopped, her hand poised in midair.

She stared openmouthed at the pair of scissors on top of her clothing.

Scissors?

She picked them up with a trembling hand.

She brought them close to her face to examine them.

There were strands of straight black hair caught on the blades.

Hannah's straight black hair

Chapter 8

A Confession

Corky sat by herself at the far end of the table, staring down at her bowl as the corn flakes turned to mush. The brightly lit dining hall echoed with excited voices and laughter, but she didn't hear them.

At the other end of the table Kimmy, Debra, Ronnie, and Heather ate quickly, downing stacks of pancakes and french toast, spooning up bowls of cereal as they talked enthusiastically. They all kept glancing down the table at Corky, but she lowered her eyes, avoiding their curious stares.

Turning her eyes to the food line, Corky saw Hannah approach Miss Green, who had just entered and was standing near the back wall. Miss Green, her arms crossed over the chest of her gray sweatshirt, had a grim expression on her face and kept shaking her head. Hannah was talking rapidly, her face flushed, gesturing wildly with the sad black braid in her hand.

Corky realized that Miss Green was staring at her, her face drawn into a tight frown.

What's going to happen now? Corky wondered, a heavy feeling of dread in the pit of her stomach. What is Miss Green going to do to Kimmy and me?

What should *I* do? Corky asked herself. Should I tell her that Kimmy cut off the braid? Should I tell her that Kimmy put the scissors in my dresser drawer to make it look as if I had done it? Should I tell her that Kimmy is inhabited by the evil spirit?

I have to tell someone, Corky thought glumly, hearing a burst of loud laughter from the girls at the next table. I can't let Kimmy go any further.

Hannah was still talking furiously, waving the braid in the air, pacing back and forth in front of Miss Green as she talked.

Just then the Bulldog cheerleaders erupted in a long cheer. Corky turned her eyes to their table to see Blair O'Connell, a peppy smile on her face, energetically leading the chant.

Doesn't she *ever* quit? Corky thought bitterly.

The cheerleaders were supposed to show pep and spirit every moment of the day, from the time they woke up in the morning. But give me a *break!* Corky thought, shaking her head. She dropped her spoon into the soggy cereal with a *plop*.

The cheer ended at the Bulldogs' table, and another cheer, even louder, erupted at the next table. Corky noticed that Hannah had returned to the Shadyside table, taking her place beside Debra. She was red faced and looked as if she'd been crying. She and Debra were whispering together.

Kimmy was at the head of the table, chewing on a slice of buttered toast, her expression troubled. Heather leaned forward then to ask Kimmy a question, but Kimmy didn't seem to hear her.

The evil is here at this table, Corky thought, staring hard at Kimmy. Corky shuddered. Two other cheers started up just then at two different tables. The shouting voices echoed off the yellow tile walls and high ceilings.

Corky suddenly felt terribly frightened. And terribly alone.

Who can I talk to? she asked herself. Who can I confide in? Debra would understand, she realized. Debra knew all about the evil spirit. Debra had been changed by it too.

Corky pushed her chair back and climbed to her feet. Ignoring the happy cheers at the other tables, she edged her way down the aisle and stopped behind Debra.

"Debra—can I talk to you?" she asked, bending down so that Debra could hear her over the shouting voices.

Debra turned around slowly. "Hi, Corky. Can it wait?" Debra asked, shouting over the noise. "I'm talking to Hannah right now."

Stung by Debra's words, Corky stepped back.

Ignoring Corky, Debra leaned close to Hannah as the two of them continued to whisper together.

Surely Debra can see that I'm upset, that I've been sitting off by myself, Corky thought angrily. What kind of friend is she?

And since when is Hannah so important to Debra that Debra can't interrupt her conversation to talk to me when I really need her?

On the verge of tears, Corky started toward the dining hall door. I can't deal with this, she thought. I've got to get out of here!

She was halfway to the door when she heard Miss Green calling to her.

Corky stopped but didn't turn around. I can't face this, she thought. This is going to be horrible.

She took a deep breath and held it. Letting it out slowly, to calm herself, she turned. Kimmy had climbed to her feet and was starting away from the table. Miss Green had called her too.

A stern expression on her face, Miss Green motioned for the girls to join her against the far wall. Corky walked slowly, her mind racing. What am I going to say? How am I going to explain?

Glancing back to the table, she saw that the four Tiger cheerleaders were staring at Kimmy and her, not talking now, just watching intently to see what would happen.

The cheers seemed to fade into the distance as Corky approached Miss Green, walking slowly, her heart thudding in her chest. She glanced at Kimmy, who was staring straight ahead, lost in her own thoughts.

"Hannah has brought a serious complaint against you two," Miss Green said without any other greeting.

She stared first at Corky, then at Kimmy, her dark eyes searching for some kind of answer. "I—I really can't believe this happened. I mean, what Hannah told me. It's just so—cruel. So incredibly vicious."

Neither Corky nor Kimmy said anything. Corky could feel her chin quivering. She tried to stop it but couldn't.

"I know both of you girls," Miss Green continued finally. "I like you both. And I—I'm just flabbergasted. That's the only word I can think of. I can't believe that either of you . . ." Her voice trailed off.

Time seemed to stand still. Corky couldn't breathe. It was as if her lungs were ready to explode.

"Cutting off someone's hair can be described only as an attack," Miss Green said sternly, narrowing her eyes at the two girls. "A truly vicious attack."

Corky lowered her eyes to her hands, which were ice cold, she realized. She had balled them into such tight fists that her fingernails were cutting into her palms.

"I have to know," Miss Green said. "I have no choice. I have to find out which of you did this terrible thing to Hannah."

She turned her hard gaze on Kimmy. "Kimmy—was it you who cut off Hannah's braid?"

Kimmy cleared her throat. "Yes," she said.

Chapter 9

The Blood Flows

Miss Green's mouth dropped open in shock. She wasn't expecting Kimmy to confess, Corky thought. At least, not that fast.

Corky turned her eyes to Kimmy, who gave her a meaningful glance. Kimmy was telling her: Go along with this. Don't contradict me—I'm covering for you.

Kimmy thinks she's protecting *me!* Corky realized. No. No way. I can't let her do this.

Kimmy is the guilty one, Corky knew. But it isn't Kimmy's fault; she isn't in control of her own body. I can't let Kimmy take the blame for this alone.

"No, Miss Green," Corky said. "I did it. I was the one."

Miss Green's face turned hard and cold. "Follow me," she said, motioning for both of them to go with her.

She led them through the double doors into the hallway. It was quiet out there, and cooler.

Miss Green stopped abruptly and spun around, anger expressed on her face. "I want the truth," she snapped. "I don't want you covering for each other. I want to know the truth. Who's responsible."

"I did it," Kimmy said in a low voice, darting a quick glance at Corky to keep quiet.

"No," Corky said, ignoring her friend. "It's not true."

"Then *you* did it?" Miss Green demanded, stepping up close to Corky, so close Corky could smell the coffee on her breath.

"No." Corky shook her head and took a deep breath. She had to tell her about the evil spirit, she decided. She really had no choice. "The truth is—"

"Yes, what *is* the truth?" Miss Green urged impatiently.

"The truth is that neither of us did it," Corky blurted out. "You see—"

"Stop!" Miss Green interrupted, holding up both hands. She sighed—a long, exasperated sigh. "I'm going to deal with both of you when we get back to Shadyside."

"Miss Green—" Corky started. But the advisor raised her hands again to cut Corky off.

"We'll do a complete investigation when we get back," Miss Green said, lowering her voice to a whisper as two of the striped-jacketed judges walked by. "When we get back to Shadyside, both of you will be disciplined. Disciplined strongly." She slowly shook her head from side to side.

"Miss Green, we're really sorry," Kimmy said softly.

"No apologies," the advisor said sharply. "Let's just try to finish the week, okay? With no further incidents? I-I'm just flabbergasted. I can't imagine what could have gotten into your heads!"

I can, Corky thought glumly.

She and Kimmy watched as Miss Green, taking a few long, angry strides, hurried back into the dining hall. Then Corky turned to Kimmy, her chin quivering again. "I—uh . . ." She couldn't think of what to say.

"This really makes me feel like going out and giving it my all," Kimmy muttered sarcastically.

"Yeah, I know," Corky agreed.

"I mean, what's the point?" Kimmy cried, throwing up her hands. "Why should we work on routines and go ahead with all of this? We're both going to be thrown off the squad when we get back to school."

Corky started to agree, but her voice caught in her throat.

"I was so psyched for this camp," Kimmy said sadly, pushing back her dark hair. "But now . . ." Her voice trailed off.

The hallway suddenly exploded with loud voices, calls, and laughter. Breakfast had ended, and everyone was heading to the gym for the morning workout.

Walking together in silence, Corky and Kimmy followed the others out onto the quadrangle. It was a bright, clear day, the sun already high in a cloudless sky.

A Frisbee sailed past Corky's head. A cheerleader in

a gold uniform, gleaming in the sunlight, leapt to catch it. Then the girl spun around and flung it back in an easy motion.

The beautiful day didn't help cheer Corky. She knew it would take more than sunlight to make her problems go away.

She and Kimmy both saw Blair O'Connell at the same time, and both stopped on the path to stare at her.

Blair was performing a set of perfect cartwheels on the grass, rolling joyfully just for the fun of it.

"She really makes me sick," Kimmy declared, leaning close so that only Corky could hear. Corky found herself startled by the angry heat of Kimmy's words.

"I mean, she *really* makes me sick," Kimmy repeated, making a disgusted face as she watched Blair's exuberant performance. "Someone should do something about her."

"We can't let the other girls down," Corky told Kimmy, pulling on the bottom of her cheerleader sweater and brushing a piece of lint off the big maroon S on the front. "We've got to give it our best."

"I guess you're right," Kimmy agreed halfheartedly.

They had practiced all afternoon, working to get a complicated new rap routine to come together. But neither of them had practiced with her usual enthusiasm and spirit.

Now it was seven-thirty, time for the evening competition. The enormous gym rang out with excited voices. Corky could *feel* the tension, could feel everyone anticipating performing in front of the judges.

Hannah and Debra were clapping and stamping their feet in rhythm, practicing. Hannah had hurried into town and returned with a new, short hairstyle—she seemed as pert as ever. Ronnie was kneeling on the floor, frantically trying to repair a broken sneaker lace. Heather was several feet away, doing leg stretches.

"The show must go on," Corky said, forcing a smile.

"Why?" Kimmy asked.

Corky shrugged. "Beats me."

They both laughed. Their first laugh of the day.

Whistles blew. The gym slowly became quiet. A judge, a young woman with striking blond hair, called the captains to the center of the floor. The captains drew straws to determine the order of the competition.

"Yaaaay, Bulldogs!" Blair O'Connell, holding a red straw, screamed.

"Guess who's going first?" Kimmy whispered sarcastically to Corky.

Corky rolled her eyes. "Blair is unreal!" she muttered.

Secretly, she admitted to herself that she was more than a little jealous of Blair. Blair was happy . . . she was having a great time . . . she was really into the competition. Blair was at her best—and she knew it.

That's the way I *used* to feel, Corky thought. That's the way Bobbi and I always felt when we were cheering. We always felt so confident, so *terrific,* so on top of everything whenever we put on our uniforms.

But now . . .

Now she could only watch Blair and the other happy, enthusiastic cheerleaders, and envy them.

"Clear the floor!" a voice cried over the loudspeaker. The cheerleaders scrambled up into the bleachers, sneakers thudding and squeaking. The eight Bulldog cheerleaders remained on the floor, huddling beside the bleachers.

Corky found a seat on the very end of a bench, about eight rows up from the floor. Debra sat beside her, nodded to her, smiling, but didn't say anything.

Corky turned away from Debra, still feeling hurt and angry by Debra's behavior toward her that morning. She looked down from her vantage point and watched Blair O'Connell encourage her squad. Blair went from girl to girl, saying something to each one.

A spotlight came on high in the ceiling rafters, throwing a white circle of light onto the gleaming, polished floor. The bleachers grew quiet.

"The Redwood Bulldogs will go first tonight," announced the voice on the loudspeaker. "Whenever you are ready . . ."

The judges raised their clipboards as if at attention.

After a long pause the Bulldogs came running out clapping from beside the bleachers. They entered in a single line, Blair O'Connell in the lead.

As Blair ran into the spotlight, she performed a handspring. She dived forward onto her hands, flipped her body over, and landed effortlessly on both feet. Still on the run, she started into a second handspring.

But as she leapt this time, she appeared to trip over something.

Startled, her eyes grew wide. Her arms flew up.

She plunged forward, falling.

Her arms flailed the air helplessly as she landed—on her face.

Corky heard the sickening *crack* as her face hit the hardwood floor.

Her arms continued to thrash about wildly, but Blair made no attempt to get up.

The silence in the gym hung heavy. The spotlight flooded her still form with glaring white light.

When Blair finally raised herself up, her eyes wild with confusion and fright, bright scarlet blood was gushing from her mouth like spurting water from a fountain.

Even from where she was sitting, Corky could see the cut in Blair's lip. And she could see that her two front teeth had been broken in half.

Blair's head rolled about as blood continued to flow from her mouth, down the front of her uniform.

Her teammates ran over to huddle around her. Two girls put their arms around her waist.

Horrified shrill voices rang out. "Where's the doctor?"

"Somebody help her!"

"Her teeth! Her teeth are broken!"

"Stop the bleeding!"

"Her lip—it's cut wide open!"

And then Blair's anguished cry rose up over the other frantic voices. "Somebody tripped me!"

At first Corky assumed she hadn't heard correctly.

But Blair repeated her accusation. "Somebody tripped me!"

The cheerleaders in the bleachers had all jumped to their feet. The rumble of distressed voices rose to a roar.

Leaving a smeared trail of blood on the floor, Blair was half carried and half walked out of the gym. The judges and Blair's teammates moved her quickly toward the medical office down the hall.

As they passed beside her, Corky heard Blair repeat her accusation, the words burbling out like the blood from her mouth. "Somebody tripped me! Somebody tripped me!"

Repeated over and over like some kind of tragic cheer.

And then Blair was gone. Only the smeared trail of blood remained under the hot white glare of the spotlight.

Corky stared at the floor until it became a white blur. Then she forced herself to lift her eyes and focus down the row on Kimmy.

To her surprise Kimmy was staring back at her, the strangest look on her face.

Chapter 10

The Scissors Again

"Let's do the diamond-head pyramid," Kimmy suggested. "That's always a winner."

Corky stared at Kimmy in surprise. The other girls cheered enthusiastically.

It was the next afternoon, a gray, overcast day of low-hovering clouds. But inside the gym spirits were as bright as ever. The afternoon practice was under way—cheerleaders in shorts and T-shirts were beginning to work on routines for the evening competition.

"Kimmy, are you sure—?" Corky started, but her words were drowned out by loud chants from the squad a few feet away.

Suddenly gripped with fear, Corky remembered the last time they had performed the diamond-head pyramid. She and Bobbi had taught the squad how to do it. It was complicated and dangerous with three girls

72

standing on the bottom, two girls standing on their shoulders, and one girl on top of them.

When they were in position, the girls all performed liberties, posing with one foot raised to their heads. Then the top girl did a tuck jump into the arms of the girl on the right end.

We haven't done the pyramid since that night, Corky thought with a shudder. The night I was on top. When I made my jump, Kimmy deliberately let me fall.

She wanted to kill me.

She was inhabited by the evil spirit and she wanted to kill me.

Why is she suggesting we do the pyramid again tonight?

"Kimmy—do you really think it's a good idea?" Corky asked, staring hard at her friend.

"Yes!"

"Let's do it!"

"Let's try!"

The others all voiced their enthusiasm.

"Let me be on top!" Hannah shouted eagerly, her pleas directed at Kimmy. "Please!"

"Okay. You're on top," Kimmy answered quickly.

Too quickly, Corky thought.

Is Kimmy planning on letting Hannah fall? Is that her plan? She's already *tortured* Hannah. Is she intending to *kill* her too?

Corky decided she had to act. She pushed her way past Ronnie, who was struggling with a shoelace, and walked up to confront Kimmy.

"What's going on?" Corky demanded. "I've always been on top in the pyramid."

73

"Let's give Hannah a chance," Kimmy replied softly, almost innocently.

"Yeah—come on, Corky, give Hannah a chance," Debra interrupted.

Wow, thought Corky, Debra has certainly become Hannah's pal in a hurry. She turned her gaze on Debra. Fingering the crystal she always wore around her neck, Debra stared at Corky as if challenging her.

"I really think I should be on top," Corky insisted, turning back to argue with Kimmy. "I mean, we only have this afternoon to practice. There really isn't time to break in someone new."

But Kimmy insisted: "Let's give Hannah a chance." And the other girls quickly agreed.

Corky backed off as Hannah flashed her a triumphant smile.

The smile cut Corky like a knife. It was a cold smile, a cruel smile. It said: I'm the star now . . . I'm the favorite now—and you're nothing. No one wants to hear *your* opinion.

Dread swept over Corky. Staring at Hannah, she had a heavy feeling in her stomach. She realized her hands had suddenly become ice cold.

Hannah is doomed. The words flashed through Corky's mind. Kimmy cannot be stopped. *Hannah is doomed.*

"Didn't you hear me?" Kimmy's shout interrupted Corky's frightening thoughts.

"S-sorry," Corky stammered. "I was just thinking . . ."

"Let's try the pyramid," Kimmy said. "We'll practice the shoulder stand—in case anyone forgot." She turned to Hannah. "Watch carefully. Corky and Debra will be in the middle. We'll help you make your climb."

"This is so exciting!" Hannah squealed.

"More exciting than you think," Corky muttered under her breath.

"Corky—did you say something?" Kimmy asked, a challenge in her voice.

Corky shook her head no and stepped forward to demonstrate the shoulder stand.

A few minutes later five girls were in position and Hannah began to make her way to the top.

Balancing on Ronnie's and Heather's shoulders, Corky felt a chill run down her back. She forced away a shiver of dizziness.

Was Kimmy planning to drop Hannah now? In practice?

Or was she going to wait until the evening competition?

She wanted to warn Hannah, to tell her the truth, to tell her about Kimmy. But what was the point? She knew that Hannah would never believe her.

Hannah reached up with her hands. Corky grabbed them and tugged. Hannah's hands were hot and wet. She was breathing noisily as she hoisted herself up and moved into position to the top of the pyramid.

"Excellent!" Miss Green called, jogging across the gym. She had arrived late, but didn't seem at all surprised to see the girls practicing the pyramid. "Hold it. Don't move!" she shouted up to them, smiling. "Hannah, don't move. Just get a feel for it—get a feel for your balance."

"I'm fine!" Hannah declared. "This is easy! Really!"

"Okay. Liberties!" Kimmy instructed.

"Slow. Take it slow. Hold your balance," Miss Green called.

Corky, Debra, Ronnie, and Kimmy slowly raised one leg each.

"Steady, Ronnie," Miss Green urged. "Keep your other knee locked. All right, legs down."

Corky could feel Hannah sway unsteadily above her.

She realized she was holding her breath. Is Kimmy going to drop Hannah? *Is* she?

Time seemed to slow, then freeze.

Corky finally exhaled, took another deep breath, and held it.

"Lean forward just before you begin your tuck jump," Miss Green was telling Hannah.

"No problem," Hannah declared.

"Debra will have to shift her weight and balance on one leg," Miss Green instructed. "Then Kimmy will step out from under her and forward to catch you."

"I get it," Hannah called out. "I'm ready."

"On three," Miss Green said, her expression set, her eyes narrowed as she stared up at Hannah. "One . . . two . . ."

Kimmy stepped forward to catch Hannah.

Corky closed her eyes.

"Three."

Corky felt the pressure on her shoulder as Hannah

pushed off for her jump. She saw Kimmy step forward.

Corky opened her eyes in time to see Kimmy catch Hannah easily.

Smiling happily, Hannah bounced to the floor, clapping.

The pyramid collapsed. Corky jumped down, feeling another shiver of dizziness.

Everyone was cheering and congratulating Hannah.

Miss Green, usually somber faced, was smiling too. "Take a five-minute break!" she called.

Corky began to make her way to the water fountain in the hall.

"Are you okay?"

She looked up to see Kimmy staring at her, concerned.

"Are you okay?" Kimmy repeated.

"Yeah, I guess," Corky replied unsteadily. I don't want a confrontation now, she thought. I can't handle a confrontation with Kimmy now. "I'm okay."

Kimmy stared at her coldly, her eyes glowing. "Good," she said. "I'm glad. I think some people are in for a surprise tonight—don't you?"

"This skirt is so wrinkled," Kimmy said, holding the maroon and white cheerleader skirt up in front of her. "Think anyone brought an iron?"

Corky, brushing her hair in front of her dresser mirror, raised her eyes to examine Kimmy in the mirror. "It doesn't look so bad."

Hannah was in the shower. Corky could hear her humming to herself over the steady rush of water.

Shaking her head, Kimmy pulled the skirt on. "We're late," she said, adjusting the bottom of her sweater over the skirt. "We're all late."

"I'm almost ready," Corky replied, setting down the hairbrush.

"What do you think is for dinner?" Kimmy asked, fluffing her black hair with both hands. "Hope it isn't chili. After dinner last night I felt like I weighed a thousand pounds—I could barely get off the floor."

"Yeah, I know," Corky replied, reaching for her lip gloss.

"I'm going down," Kimmy said, taking one last look at herself in the mirror, adjusting her skirt. "Meet you in the dining hall, okay?"

"Okay," Corky told her. "I'll only be a minute."

Kimmy hurried out. As the door slammed behind her, the bathroom door opened, and Hannah stepped out, surrounded by warm steam, wrapped in a large maroon bath towel, her newly short black hair wet and dripping.

"We're going to win tonight," she said enthusiastically. "I just know it. With Blair gone, the Bulldogs are out of it." She sat down on the bed and began rubbing her hair with the towel.

"Blair won't be cheering tonight?" Corky asked, having trouble clasping her watch on her wrist.

"No. Didn't you hear?" Hannah replied from under the bath towel. "She went home. She had ten stitches on her lip, and she's got to have dental surgery."

"Too bad," Corky said softly. She stood up and stretched.

Hannah dropped the towel, pulled on her underwear, then sat back down on the bed to put on her maroon uniform socks. Her back was to Corky.

"With Blair out of the way, we *have* to win!" Hannah declared.

Corky quickly pulled open her top drawer. Her hand fumbled through the T-shirts inside until she found the scissors.

Wrapping her hand around the handle, she lifted the scissors from the drawer.

Hannah was still talking excitedly about the competition, her back to Corky.

Raising the scissors like a knife, Corky took a step toward Hannah.

This is my chance to finish what I started, Corky thought.

Silently she made her way across the floor and stopped behind her unsuspecting roommate.

No more teasing, Corky thought. No more fooling around. This is it.

Goodbye, Hannah.

I can't say it's been a pleasure knowing you.

As Hannah leaned forward on the edge of the bed to pick up her other sock from the floor, Corky brought the scissor blade down quickly, aiming for the tender spot between Hannah's shoulder blades.

Chapter 11

Corky's Surprising Discovery

You're dead, Hannah. You're *dead!*

The door swung open.

"Would you believe I forgot the pom-poms again?" Kimmy said, hurrying in breathlessly.

Corky let the scissors drop to the carpet and quickly kicked them under Hannah's bed.

Hannah spun around, surprised to find Corky so close behind her.

Feeling her face grow hot, Corky stepped back to her bed. A strong wave of nausea rose from the pit of her stomach. She held her breath, forcing it down.

Her head spun. She saw brilliant red lights. The entire room flashed, red then black, red then black.

Still struggling to fight down her nausea, she turned to Kimmy, who was searching the front closet, "I think you shoved the box over here, by our bed," Corky said, pointing.

"Thanks." Kimmy hurried over and picked up the carton. "Hey—aren't you two ready yet? What's taking so long?"

"I'll be ready in two seconds," Hannah said, pulling on her skirt.

"I—I don't feel so hot," Corky said weakly.

"Huh?" Kimmy's mouth dropped open in surprise.

"Really," Corky insisted. "My stomach. I don't feel right." She dropped down onto the edge of her bed.

The room flashed red then black, red then black.

She had a roaring in her ears, like a rushing waterfall. The back of her neck felt prickly and hot.

"You're not coming to dinner?" Kimmy asked shrilly.

"I'll be down as soon as I feel better," Corky told her. "Tell Miss Green, okay?"

Another wave of nausea sent her running to the bathroom. She slammed the door behind her and gripped the sink with both hands. The porcelain felt cool under her hot, wet hands.

Her entire body convulsed in a powerful tremor.

Red then black. Red then black.

She shut her eyes, but the flashing colors continued on her eyelids.

The roar in her ears grew louder.

She thought she heard laughter, evil laughter, somewhere far away.

Suddenly the sink became scalding hot and, with a cry more of shock than of pain, she jerked her hands away.

Steam rose from the empty sink, putrid and thick, smelling of mold and decay. The porcelain shim-

81

mered and melted from the heat as she gaped in disbelief at it.

A hideous, low, gurgling sound rose from the drain, growing louder and louder until it became a moan.

Corky turned and ran. She burst out of the bathroom and threw herself down on Hannah's bed.

The room was empty. Hannah and Kimmy were gone.

I nearly killed Hannah, Corky realized. I nearly murdered her.

And then the horrifying words pushed their way into her consciousness:

I am the evil one now.

PART TWO

Cold Fear

Chapter 12

Using Her Powers

Back in Shadyside, Corky could barely remember the last days of camp. Everything was a blur since she had discovered the awful truth. This Saturday afternoon found Corky in her room.

"Corky, what are you doing?" Her mother's concerned voice called through the closed door.

"Just resting," Corky called back, raising her head from the pillow. Dressed in faded jeans and a sleeveless yellow T-shirt, she had thrown herself onto her bed after lunch. Thoughts washed about in her head like unruly ocean waves—strange thoughts, thoughts that weren't entirely her own.

"Are you sick?" her mother called in. "It's not like you to rest on a Saturday afternoon."

"I'm just tired," Corky replied impatiently. "You know . . . from cheerleader camp."

She listened to her mother pad down the stairs. Then she buried her head deep in the pillow, trying to drown out the roaring in her ears.

Cheerleader camp. What a dreadful week.

She stayed in her dorm room after she had made her horrifying discovery. She told everyone she was sick.

What choice did she have?

She couldn't go to any of the workshops or practices; she couldn't perform in the evening competitions. She was too afraid she might hurt someone.

Or worse.

She had stayed in bed when Kimmy or Hannah were in the room. She tried to talk to them as little as possible.

Miss Green got a doctor to come examine Corky. But, of course, he found nothing wrong.

Nothing wrong. What a laugh, she thought bitterly.

Sometimes the evil force faded a little. Sometimes it let her think clearly. Sometimes it gave her just enough time to herself to become afraid, truly afraid.

And then the roar, the endless roar would return, and her memories would leave her. And she would move in a world of deep red and darker black, and not remember.

Not remember anything at all.

Except the fear.

Lying on top of her bedcovers, tossing uncomfortably, feeling the weight of the ancient evil, she remembered everything now.

So clearly. Too clearly.

She remembered sitting in the coffeeshop with the other girls, making the pea soup spurt up over the table.

Why? Because they had teased her. And just because she *could.*

She remembered reaching out across the gym, reaching, reaching to trip Blair O'Connell. What a pleasing sight that was. And what a pleasing sound. That *crack.* That *crunch.* The sound of her face hitting the floor, her teeth breaking.

How satisfying, the shimmering red blood that flowed from her wounded mouth.

And there was more. More!

She remembered getting up in the early hours of morning, the sky still heavy with night. She remembered creeping to the desk drawer and silently removing her scissors. She remembered working carefully to cut off Hannah's disgusting black braid. She remembered the soft, nearly silent *snip snip* as she moved the blade through the thick hair. And she remembered placing the severed braid neatly on top of Hannah's covers so she would see it the moment she woke up.

That was fun.

But later her fun had been interrupted.

Kimmy burst in to spoil her fun, spoil her chance to murder Hannah.

That had made her so angry the roar had drowned out all her thoughts. She had disappeared inside herself, somewhere far away.

And now . . . now . . .

Corky sat up, uttering a low cry.

She suddenly understood the dreams, the dreams about Bobbi.

She suddenly understood what Bobbi had been trying to tell her in those sickening, awful dreams.

When Bobbi had opened her skull and pointed to the horrors inside, Bobbi was telling Corky: *Look inside your own head. Look inside yourself. The horror is inside YOU!*

"Now I understand, Bobbi," Corky said out loud.

And as she said this, her bed rose. She grabbed the covers as the bed began to writhe and toss like a bus on a bumpy road.

No. Oh no. Please—nooooo.

The foot of the bed bucked as if trying to throw her off. Then the covers began to roll over her, the bed trembling and shaking.

No. Oh, please. Stop!

She clung to the bedspread, tightening her grip, holding on for dear life. The headboard slapped loudly against the wall. The covers flapped as if being blown by a hurricane wind. The mattress buckled and bumped.

Help me! Please—stop it! STOP it!

Terrified, she rolled off the bed and toppled onto the floor.

As she hit the floor, landing on her elbows and knees, the carpet began to undulate in waves, rising then buckling back down, flapping noisily.

The curtains beside her windows flew straight out as if reaching for her. The windows rose then slammed down.

Please—stop! STOP!

Her perfume bottles and cosmetics flew up from her dresser top and hovered near the ceiling.

The windows opened and shut more rapidly as the curtains continued to flap wildly. Struggling to her feet, Corky was tossed helplessly about by the rocking, undulating carpet.

She reached up toward her dresser, but the moving carpet pulled her back. The mirror above the dresser burst into flames, then appeared to melt. She gaped in open-mouthed horror as the silvery lava poured down over the front of the dresser onto the throbbing, bucking floor.

And then she saw the puddle of dark blood on the carpet just in front of her.

"Please—SOMEBODY! Please, stop!"

As she stared down at it, struggling to focus her eyes, the puddle began to bubble and then expand. The dark wetness crept wider until it was underneath her, until it spread over the throbbing carpet, until she was *swimming* in it.

Drowning in it. Drowning in the thick dark blood . . . thrashing her arms and legs . . . kicking frantically . . . trying to swim . . . but feeling herself pulled down, sucked down into the bubbling, dark ooze.

"Noooooooooooo!"

Thrashing wildly, Corky struggled to keep her head up as the blood bubbled, red waves rocking and crashing over her, sweeping her away, pulling her down.

"Why are you doing this to me? Why are you torturing me? Leave me ALONE!"

Was she screaming the words? Or only thinking them?

The bedroom door opened.

Someone stood over her.

Panting loudly, she raised her eyes.

"Sean!"

Her little brother stared at her, hands in his jeans pockets, his blue eyes wide with surprise. "What's going on? What are you doing down there?"

Gripping the carpet tightly between her fingers, crouched on all fours, Corky stared up at him.

"Man, you're messed up!" he exclaimed, laughing.

"I . . . uh . . . I guess I had a bad dream," Corky explained weakly. She pulled herself up to her knees.

Red then black. Red then black.

The roar in her ears was a steady rush in the background.

She let her eyes dart around the room.

Normal. Everything was back to normal.

Of course.

"Come to my room," Sean demanded, grabbing her hand and tugging it.

"Why?" she asked. The roar grew louder. Closer.

"I want to show you something." He tugged harder. "Something I did on the computer."

She tried to stand up, but the dizziness pushed her down.

Her head weighed a thousand pounds. The roar drowned out her thoughts.

Red then black. Then red again.

90

The world was only two colors.

"Come *on!*" Sean cried impatiently.

And suddenly, without realizing it, she was hugging him, holding on to him, pulling him close. Closer. Holding on to him because he was real. Because he was good. So good.

"Hey—what's the big idea?" he cried, trying to squirm out of her grasp.

The roar made everything vibrate, every breath echo loudly in her mind.

Red then black. Then red. Then black.

Holding on to Sean, she wrestled him playfully to the carpet.

He laughed and squirmed. He reached up and put a headlock on her with his bony arms.

Sean liked to wrestle.

She ducked out of his hold and grabbed a slender arm. I can break his arm, Corky thought. Yes. I can break both his arms.

It would be so easy. So easy to just snap them in two.

YESSSSSSS, said the roar, the insistent roar in her head.

It would be so easy.

Crack crack.

YESSSSSSSSS.

Feeling the strength, the awesome strength of her powers, Corky grabbed Sean's arm and started to bend it back.

Chapter 13

"We Have to Kill the Others"

Corky bent Sean's slender arm behind his back.

"Ow!" he protested, struggling to free himself. "You're *hurting* me!"

He wasn't strong enough to loosen her grip. She pulled the arm up, listening for the shoulder to crack.

"Ow! Stop!" Sean screamed.

She bent the arm up even more. Then, suddenly, she let go, and Sean burst free.

"Get out!" Corky screamed to her startled brother. "Get out! Get out *now!*"

He ran to the door, his blue eyes wide, his expression bewildered. Turning, he glared back at her. "What's your problem, jerk?"

"Get out, Sean! Get *out!*"

He tossed his blond hair back angrily. "First you

want to wrestle. Then you kick me out. You're a jerk!"

"Just get out," she moaned, feeling her entire body start to tremble.

He was already out the door and heading down the stairs.

I almost hurt him, Corky thought, terrified. I almost broke his arm.

Somehow the evil backed off just before . . . before . . .

She heard laughter, cold and dry. Almost a cough.

Corky glanced around the room. But she knew immediately that the laughter was inside her head.

It grew louder. Cruel laughter, taunting her. She covered her ears with her hands. Pressing hard, she tried to shut the evil sound out. But it grew louder still.

"Leave me alone! Leave me alone!" she screamed, not recognizing her own voice.

She fell onto her bed and pulled the pillow down over her head.

But the cold, dark laughter inside her mind grew louder and louder.

Corky dreamed that she was on a boat. She could feel the gentle swaying, the rise and fall of the wooden deck beneath her feet.

It was a bright day, sunny and warm. The cloudless sky was a vivid blue. The sun, reflected in the water, sent trickles of gold leaping around the white boat.

Corky could see herself standing on the swaying deck, leaning gently against the polished rail. She was dressed all in white. Her dress, floor-length and old-fashioned, had long sleeves with lacy cuffs. The skirt billowed in the soft wind. The frilly top had a high-necked lacy collar. On her head she wore a wide-brimmed straw hat with a red ribbon around the crown tied in a bow to hang long down her back.

How strange, Corky thought, to be in the dream and be able to watch the dream at the same time.

The colors were all so lovely. The sparkling gold-blue water, the white pleasure boat, the pale sky, her shimmering dress.

There were two children with her, slender and blond, also dressed in white Victorian clothes. Very dressy, Corky thought. Not for sailing.

The boat slid gently through the shimmering, calm waters.

The children called her Sarah.

The sun felt warm on her face.

I'm not me, Corky thought. I'm someone called Sarah.

"Sarah, watch me," the little boy said. He hoisted himself onto the deck rail and struck a brave pose.

"Get down from there," Sarah scolded gently, laughing despite herself. "Get down at once."

The boy obediently hopped down.

Corky watched him chase the little girl along the bright deck.

Sarah lifted her face to the sun.

Suddenly the boat heeled hard to the right. Sarah grabbed the deck rail to steady herself, to stop herself from toppling over.

What's happening? Corky wondered, feeling Sarah's alarm.

Why is the boat tilting?

The boat lurched then heeled up in the other direction. Sarah clung tightly to the rail.

She could feel the fear creep up her back.

The boat began to spin rapidly as if caught in some kind of whirlpool.

What's happening? Where is the sun? Why are we spinning like this?

The sky was suddenly black, as black as the swirling, frothing waters that lapped up noisily against the twirling boat.

Corky felt Sarah's fear. It washed over her, weighing her down, freezing her in place.

"Sarah! Sarah!" the children's voices, tiny and frightened, called to her.

She grabbed the deck rail with both hands now.

But the rail was no longer a rail. It had transformed itself into a thick white snake.

The snake raised its head, opened its venomous jaws and started to hiss at Sarah. . . .

Then Corky woke up.

Drenched in cold perspiration, she sat up straight, gasping for air. She blinked and rubbed her eyes, rubbing away the vision of the hideous hissing snake.

I'm back, she thought. Back in my room.

The dream had been so real. It hadn't felt like a dream. More like a memory. A powerful memory.

She looked over at her bedside clock. Seven-thirty. Outside her windows, the sky was the color of charcoal.

I've slept right through dinner, Corky realized.

What a frightening dream.

But why did it seem so familiar, almost as if she had lived it before.

And why had the children called her Sarah?

Still feeling shaky, still feeling the frightening pull of the boat as it spun, Corky lowered her feet to the floor.

She opened her mouth in a wide yawn.

And as she yawned, she heard a hissing sound—the hissing of the snake?—like a strong, unending wind escaping from deep within her.

She tried to close her mouth, but it wouldn't close.

The hissing grew louder, and Corky could feel something pour from her mouth.

A disgusting, putrid odor invaded her nose as green gas spewed from her open mouth.

From inside me! she thought in horror. And I can't stop it.

She sat helplessly as the green gas poured out of her mouth, filling the room with its powerful stench.

Help me. Oh, help me!

I can't stop it. I can't close my mouth.

It smells so bad!

The green gas roared out of her mouth. More. And more.

I'm going to vomit forever. Forever! Corky thought, her entire body trembling as the green gas spewed out.

When it was finally out, the hissing stopped. Weak, Corky fell back against her headboard, dizzy and drained.

The room was filled with the putrid mist. It hovered hot and wet, like a heavy fog.

"Don't sit back. We have work to do," said a voice that crackled like wind through dry leaves.

"Huh? Work? What w-work?" Corky managed to stammer breathlessly, pressed up against her headboard, trembling violently, unable to stop her body from shuddering.

"We have to kill the others, the ones who betrayed you," whispered the voice in the disgusting green fog. "Let's start with Debra."

Chapter 14

Killing Debra

"**N**o!" Corky screamed in a high-pitched voice she'd never heard before.

She pressed her back against the headboard, trying to escape the foul odor, the smoky green shadow that hovered over the room. Shaking all over, chills rolling down her back, she realized that her room had become icy cold.

"I won't kill Debra," Corky insisted, crossing her arms protectively over the front of her T-shirt. She stared hard at the shadow as it billowed silently in front of her.

"But Debra turned against you. She chose Hannah over you," came the dry whisper. "Now Debra must pay."

"No! I won't let you!" Corky screamed shrilly.

The evil voice laughed, dry laughter like breaking

twigs. "You won't let me?" The heavy mist rose up toward the ceiling. "But you *are* me!"

"No!" Corky protested.

"You are me—and I am you!"

"No! Please!"

The voice laughed again. The green fog folded in on itself, billowing and bending in the dark, cold room.

And then it floated rapidly up to the ceiling.

Her entire body shuddering violently, gripped in panic, Corky's breath caught in her throat. She stared in horror as the green gas spread over the ceiling, blanketing the light fixture to darken the room.

Corky grabbed her bedspread and pulled it up to her chin.

She thought of burrowing beneath it—but she knew that it wouldn't hide her from this powerful evil.

Above her the gas bubbled and billowed. Then, suddenly, it began to rain down on Corky, a heavy green dew, foul-smelling and damp.

Corky closed her eyes and covered her face with both hands.

The heavy dew descended over her, smothered her with its odor. Heavier. Heavier. Weighing her down as if it were a heavy old quilt.

I can't breathe, she thought. It's *suffocating* me.

Heavier. Heavier.

She felt so sleepy. So far away. The room seemed to fade into the distance. *She* seemed to fade with it.

As the sickening green liquid fell on her, Corky was floating away from herself.

Floating, floating into grayness.

Floating far away as the green gas filled her up, filled her mind, took over her body.

In a short while Corky was gone.

The evil force was completely in control.

She stood up, straightened her T-shirt, and walked over to her phone, taking long, steady strides.

Picking up the receiver, she punched in Debra's number. A few seconds later Debra was on the other end.

"Can you meet me?" Corky asked calmly. "I have something important to tell you."

Debra agreed.

Corky pulled a brush through her hair, then hurried downstairs. She grabbed up the car keys and called to her parents that she'd be back in a few hours.

Then she headed out to kill Debra.

Chapter 15

So Easy to Kill

Gripping the steering wheel tightly in both hands, Corky leaned forward against the shoulder belt and headed the blue Accord along Old Mill Road in the direction of the Division Street mall.

I'm coming, Debra, she thought.

I'm coming to get you.

A smile passed across her face as she blinked her eyes in the white glare of oncoming headlights.

Debra and Hannah. They were quite a team at camp. Just about inseparable.

Well, I think I can separate you now, Corky thought darkly. I think the grave will separate you from your pal Hannah!

The thought pleased Corky greatly as she remembered how Debra had refused to interrupt her conversation with Hannah to come talk with her. How

Debra went everywhere with Hannah, forgetting entirely about Corky. How Debra defended Hannah. How Debra voted that Hannah should have the top spot on the pyramid.

Debra, Debra, Debra. What a bad choice you made, Corky thought.

She sped up to pass a slow-moving station wagon filled with kids. Shadows rolled across her smiling face as the tall street lamps whirred past.

After waiting at the stoplight, she made a left onto Division Street, unexpectedly crowded with cars inching along.

Debra had explained over the phone that she had to pick up some things for her mother at the mall. "Mom had kids just so she'd have slaves," Debra had complained. "That's all she does ever since I got my driver's license—sends me off to the mall to buy stuff for her."

Corky had tsk-tsked sympathetically, thinking all the while about how much she was going to enjoy seeing the end of Debra. Debra and her cold blue eyes. Debra and that chic short haircut. Debra and that goofy crystal she was always fingering as if it had some strange power.

Power? What a laugh. I'll show her *power,* Corky thought gleefully.

She had arranged to meet Debra in the far corner of the parking lot in back of the big Dalby's department store. No one parked back there, Corky knew, unless the rest of the lot was filled. It would most likely be deserted this time of night.

Corky turned the Accord into the mall and headed

for the back. She saw two boys from school standing at the ticket window to the sixplex movie theater.

She stopped to let a woman pushing a filled shopping cart pass, then continued behind the department store.

This vast lot was nearly deserted, dotted only with cars that probably belonged to store workers.

Corky's eyes eagerly roamed the dimly lit lot.

Yes. There was Debra. Standing in a puddle of gray light, all alone at the back of the lot, her hands stuffed in her jeans pockets.

This is so easy, Corky thought. So totally *easy!*

Aiming the car at Debra, she pushed her foot down hard on the gas pedal. All the way down!

The car lurched forward with a roar.

Debra, staring at the other end of the lot, didn't notice her at first.

Then her mouth dropped open in a silent scream and her eyes bulged with fright as she realized the blue Accord was roaring at her.

So easy, Corky thought gleefully. This is *so easy!*

Chapter 16

Try, Try Again

$\mathbf{A}$s the car roared toward its target, Corky leaned forward against the shoulder belt, her eyes glowing with anticipation, her lips twisted in a triumphant grin.

Captured in the twin white headlights, Debra's face was a perfect portrait of horror.

She knows she's dead, Corky thought gleefully.

She can already feel it. She can already feel the car as it crushes her, the pain coursing through her body, the gasping for breath that won't come.

Die, Debra! Die!

As the car roared toward collision, Debra leapt away. Out of the light. Onto a low concrete divider.

Corky's car slammed into the divider with a deafening *crunch*. Then it bounced off and lurched into a lamppost.

"Ooof!"

Corky was jolted hard: forward so that the steering wheel shot into her chest, then back, her head slamming against the headrest with jarring force.

She stared straight ahead into the darkness, waiting for the pain to stop shooting through her body.

Silence.

The engine must have cut off.

Where's Debra? Corky wondered, unfastening the seat belt.

Did she get away?

The pain melted quickly. The ancient powers pushed the pain away.

Maybe Debra is under the car, Corky thought hopefully.

Loud, insistent tapping on the window beside her head startled her. She turned to see Debra, alive and healthy, tapping with one hand, a worried look on her face. "Corky—are you okay? Are you hurt?"

Sighing in disappointment, Corky pushed open the car door. "I'm okay." She climbed out into the sultry night air.

"What *happened?*" Debra demanded. "I—I was so scared. I thought you were going to mow me down!"

"The accelerator stuck," Corky told her. "I couldn't get the car to slow down. I—I completely lost control."

"How awful!" Debra exclaimed. Impulsively, she hugged Corky. "You're really okay? You hit that post pretty hard!"

Corky took a step back and examined the car. The left bumper had been crushed in. "Dad'll have a cow!" she said, shaking her head.

"But you're okay? Your head? Your neck?" Debra's face revealed her concern.

"I'm fine. Really," Corky replied impatiently. "How about you?"

"My heart is still racing, but I'm fine," Debra told her.

"Get in," Corky said, motioning toward the passenger door. "I've got to talk to you. It's pretty important."

"Maybe we should call a tow truck or your dad or something," Debra suggested.

"No. The car will probably still drive," Corky said, lowering her eyes to the damaged bumper. "I'll test it. Come on, get in. This is important."

"Why don't we take my car?" Debra insisted, pointing to her red Geo on the other side of the divider.

"I want to try *my* car," Corky snapped angrily. "I'll drop you off at your car when we're finished—okay?"

Debra stared at her intently. "Wow, Corky—I've never seen you like this."

"Well, I'm very worried about Kimmy, and I need to talk to you," Corky said. She lowered herself back into the driver's seat and slammed the door shut. Drumming her fingers on the steering wheel, she waited while Debra made her way around the car and climbed into the passenger seat, a thoughtful expression on her pretty face.

"Kimmy? What about Kimmy?" Debra asked. "I talked to her this afternoon. She seemed fine."

Corky didn't reply. She turned the key, and the

engine started right up. Turning her head to the back window, she eased the car away from the divider.

"The car's okay now?" Debra asked. "The gas pedal—it's—"

"It's fine," Corky told her, shifting into Drive and heading toward the mall exit. "Isn't that strange?"

"Yeah," Debra agreed, studying Corky. "I'm glad. That was a close one." A nervous giggle escaped her throat.

"I was so scared," Corky said, heading the car back in the direction she had come.

"Where are we going?" Debra asked, turning to face the front, pulling on her seat belt.

"Let's go to the old mill," Corky suggested. "It's so quiet there. A good place to talk."

Debra seemed reluctant. "That broken-down old mill? It's completely falling apart."

"It's quiet," Corky repeated.

A good place to kill you, Debra.

"Are you feeling better?" Debra asked, her eyes on the shadowy trees rolling past in the darkness. "I mean, since cheerleader camp. We were all so worried about you."

"That was weird, wasn't it?" Corky said. "It must have been a virus or something. Some kind of bug."

"But you're okay now?"

Corky shrugged. "I guess. I still feel a little knocked out. I completely vegged out this afternoon . . . took a long nap. Like a two-year-old. Would you believe it?"

Debra tsk-tsked. They drove in silence for a few moments. "When you were sick at camp, Hannah did such a good job of taking up the slack," Debra gushed. "I wish you could have seen her. She was awesome."

Corky nodded but didn't reply.

"What about Kimmy?" Debra demanded a short while later, turning in her seat to stare at Corky.

"We have to do something," Corky said, lowering her voice. "I'm just so scared."

She turned off Old Mill Road onto the gravel path that led through the trees to the deserted mill.

"You mean—?" Debra started, her lips forming an *O* of surprise.

"You still have all those books on the occult?" Corky asked.

The deserted mill, a two-story wooden structure with a tall wheel at one side, rose up in the headlights. Corky cut the engine and the lights and pushed open her car door.

"Yeah, I still have them." Debra reached reflexively for the crystal she wore on a chain around her neck. "I'm still really interested in all that stuff. But—"

Corky's sneakers crunched over the gravel as she led the way to the mill and the almost dry stream beside it. She was pleased to see there were no other cars there—Shadyside students often used the mill as a place to make out.

The fresh spring leaves rustled in the trees behind them. The air was fragrant and soft. The old mill loomed in front of them, black against a dark purple sky. A sliver of pale moon was cut in half by a wisp of black cloud.

"Do you think—I mean, do you think the evil spirit

is in Kimmy again?" Debra asked reluctantly, hurrying to catch up to Corky.

"I think so," Corky replied somberly. Taking longer strides, she made her way past a broken gate, stepping over the fallen door, and walked into the old mill yard.

"That's *horrible!*" Debra exclaimed breathlessly. "Hey, Corky—wait up!"

Ignoring Debra's plea, Corky picked up her pace. Stepping over loose boards and other debris, she made her way across the yard to the towering mill wheel. It stood like a black Ferris wheel against the purple sky.

"Corky—where are you going?" Debra demanded. She had to jog to catch up. "I thought you wanted to talk."

"It's all so scary," Corky said, gazing up to the top of the rigid old wooden wheel. She raised her hands and gripped a wooden slat just above her head. "It feels good to use up some energy . . . nervous energy. You know."

"Hey, Corky, stop," Debra said, breathing hard. "I don't feel like climbing tonight."

Corky had already hoisted herself onto the wheel and was pulling herself up slat by slat to the top. The owners had locked the wheel so it no longer moved.

Climbing the wheel was a popular sport among Shadyside teenagers. Sometimes they had races to see who could get up to the top first. Sometimes kids did a high-wire act, walking along the top of the wheel with their arms straight out, balancing precariously as they moved. Sometimes they had competitions to see how many people they could squeeze on the top.

"Hey, Corky—this is dangerous," Debra protested.

Corky, halfway up the wheel, was pleased to see that her companion was following. She began to climb even quicker.

"Corky—stop! It's slippery on this thing . . . from the rain yesterday. Corky! Why do we have to climb up here?" Debra cried.

Corky pulled herself up to the top of the wheel and stood up. Stretching, she glanced around. Great view, she thought. She could see the dried-up stream and entire mill yard, cluttered with trash and broken boards. Beyond the high fence, her car parked at the end of the gravel path. Beyond that, dark trees.

Darkness. Darkness stretching forever.

She reached down and helped Debra climb onto the top. Debra rested her knees on the damp wood, then reluctantly got to her feet. "This is dumb," she said, catching her breath.

"Great view," Corky replied softly, staring out at the trees.

"You said you wanted to talk," Debra complained, shaking her head. "We could talk on the ground too, you know?"

"You afraid of heights?" Corky asked, turning her eyes on Debra.

"No. Not really."

You *should* be, Corky thought, studying her friend. You *should* be very afraid of heights, Debra.

"Why are we up here?" Debra asked, leaning forward, bending her knees and resting her hands on her thighs.

"To get a different perspective," Corky replied seriously.

"Huh?"

"I don't know." Corky shrugged, smiling. "I feel *safer* up here. Weird, huh?"

"Safer? You mean from Kimmy?" Debra asked, wrinkling her forehead.

"Yeah, from Kimmy. From everything," Corky told her.

A gust of warm air fluttered through Corky's hair. She edged closer to Debra, balancing carefully.

"Well, I don't know what to say about Kimmy," Debra said, still hunched forward. "It's all so frightening."

That's okay, thought Corky. You won't have to be frightened anymore.

Bye, Debra. It's been nice knowing you. Have a nice flight. And happy landings.

She reached out both hands and grabbed Debra's shoulders to push her over the side.

Chapter 17

Something to Look Forward To

As Corky put her hands on Debra's shoulders, Debra smiled up at her, unaware of her intentions. "I'm okay," she said.

No, you're not, thought Corky. You're not okay. You're dead. She tensed her arm muscles and started to push.

"Hey, you girls—get down from there!"

The man's voice startled Corky back.

"Oh!" she cried out, and nearly toppled off the wheel.

"Get down!" the man shouted angrily. A bright light from a flashlight invaded Corky's face, then darted over to Debra. "Don't you know it's dangerous?"

Corky squinted down to see a man in a sweatshirt and denim overalls, staring up at them, moving his flashlight from one to the other.

"We're not doing anything!" Debra called down.

"You're trespassing," the man yelled up. "Now, get down before I call the police."

"Okay, okay. We're coming," Debra said. She lowered herself to a sitting position. Then flipping over onto her stomach, she carefully climbed down the side.

Corky remained standing at the top, her anger surging, the ancient evil rising up until her entire body felt as if it were on fire.

I'm going to explode! she thought. Then I'm going to twist that guy's head around until I hear his neck crack. Then I'll rip his head off and pull the brains out through the neck.

The angry thoughts crackled like electricity in her mind.

But staring down at Debra as she made her way slowly to the ground, Corky's fury cooled. Why waste my time on that idiot? she thought.

Debra's my real target. Debra is the one who must die.

Corky lowered herself quickly down the side of the old mill wheel. Stepping onto the soft ground, she glowered at the man with the flashlight.

"I know you young people think you'll live forever," he said, keeping the light on her face, "but you really shouldn't test your luck up there."

I *will* live forever! Corky thought, feeling her anger begin to seethe again. But she kept herself under control. "You can skip the lecture," she said dryly, then hurried to catch up with Debra, who was already crunching over the gravel to the car.

A short while later Corky dropped Debra off at her car in the deserted parking lot behind the mall.

"We didn't really get to talk," Debra said quietly, pushing open the car door.

"I'll kill you tomorrow," Corky told her.

Debra's eyes opened wide. "Huh? What did you say?"

"I said I'll call you tomorrow," Corky replied, realizing her slip.

"Oh." Debra's eyes narrowed again. She giggled nervously. "I guess I didn't hear you right." She gave Corky a wave and slammed the door behind her.

You heard right. I'll kill you tomorrow, Corky thought. Something to look forward to. I'll kill you tomorrow, Debra, she thought, turning and heading the car toward the exit.

Then Kimmy will have to die.

Kimmy knows too much. Way too much.

And all that knowledge is a *dangerous* thing.

So, goodbye, Debra. And goodbye, Kimmy. Goodbye, cheerleaders. I'm afraid that from now on, *I'll* be the only one with something to cheer about.

Corky chuckled to herself, pleased with her amusing thoughts.

So much to look forward to, she told herself, turning onto Fear Street, heading for home.

Hannah's smiling face flashed into her mind.

"Don't worry, Hannah," Corky said aloud. "I haven't forgotten you. I'll be looking in on you real soon . . . to finish what I started."

Chapter 18

Sinking Deep

Corky awoke. Wide-awake. Alert. She saw the brass light fixture with its white globe above her head. The curtains, hanging straight and still in front of the dark windows. The hairbrush resting on the edge of the dresser top.

Everything was so clear. In such sharp focus. As if all that had come before had been a blur, a dream.

She sat straight up and gazed at her bed table clock. Three-oh-seven. The middle of the night.

What had awakened her? And why did she feel so . . . light?

Something is different, Corky realized. Something has changed.

Pale shadows flitted over the ceiling. They were so clear, so amazingly clear.

And then Corky realized.

The evil spirit was gone.

She was herself again. Seeing things for herself. Thinking her own thoughts.

I'm me! she thought.

It's gone! It's really gone!

Excitedly, she pushed down the covers and started to jump up.

But a heavy feeling held her back. A feeling she couldn't locate. A presence. Somewhere . . . somewhere inside her.

She sank back onto the bed.

It's still there, she knew. Is it sleeping?

Did the ancient evil have to sleep too?

How long do I have? she wondered sadly. How long do I have before it awakens and takes over again? And I am back to being a prisoner, an unwilling prisoner inside my own body?

Thoughts raced through her mind. Desperate, frightened thoughts. Corky closed her eyes and took a deep breath.

How can I get rid of it? she asked herself. How can I get my body back again . . . before I kill my friends?

The evil stirred within her. Stirred but didn't waken.

When it's awake, it's like I'm dreaming, Corky thought. I'm asleep somewhere, somewhere in my own body. Dreaming everything that's really happened.

She thought suddenly of her dream. She was on the pretty sailboat, in the long white dress. Sailing on the sparkling gold water.

And the children called her Sarah.

Sarah . . . Sarah *Fear?*

Corky struggled to remember the story of Sarah Fear.

Months before, a strange young woman named Sarah Beth Plummer, a descendant of Sarah Fear, had told Corky the story. Or part of it before she had left town.

Sarah Fear, Corky remembered, was a young woman who lived in the late 1800s. She, too, had been inhabited by the evil spirit. In the summer of 1898 she had gone sailing on Fear Lake. A beautiful, calm day. But her pleasure boat capsized, and all aboard—including Sarah—drowned.

Yes. Corky knew this story. This story had formed her dream.

Only it wasn't really a dream. It was a small chunk of memory. A small chunk of Sarah Fear's memory.

Is that crazy? Corky asked herself. Is it possible that Sarah Fear's memory was revealed to me while I slept?

It *had* to be a memory, she decided. It was too clear, too *real* to be a dream.

Excited by these thoughts, Corky climbed out of bed and started to pace back and forth over her bedroom carpet.

What does the dream mean? Why did I dream it? How did I get inside Sarah Fear's life?

Again she could feel the sleeping evil stir.

She stopped pacing. Waited. Not breathing.

It continued to sleep.

Breathless with excitement, she sat down gently on the edge of the bed. She pictured Sarah Fear in her wide-brimmed straw hat and her long white dress, leaning on the rail of the gently bobbing sailboat.

How did I see all that? Corky wondered, closing her eyes and trying to see it all again. How did I see it so clearly?

Poor Sarah Fear. She had been inhabited by the evil spirit until she died.

Corky opened her eyes, excited by a new thought.

The spirit inhabited her—and it kept her memory.

The evil force must have Sarah Fear's memories inside it, Corky realized. It must have *all* the memories of all the people it inhabited over the years.

It took over their minds. It *possessed* their minds. And that meant that it also possessed their *memories*.

So somewhere deep within the mind of the ancient evil spirit, somewhere deep inside that sleeping evil, Sarah Fear's memory remained.

And a little bit of it had escaped, had come to Corky while she slept.

How can I get to the rest of it? Corky asked herself. How can I get back into Sarah Fear's mind?

She stopped, suddenly chilled.

Why do I want to get into poor Sarah Fear's memories? What would be the point? Sarah Fear died almost a hundred years ago.

As quickly as she asked herself the questions, Corky knew the answers.

Sarah Fear had been the only one to *defeat* the evil spirit.

When Sarah Fear died, the evil spirit went to the grave with her. And the evil had remained inside her grave for nearly a hundred years.

I want to send the evil force to its grave, Corky

118

thought, breathing hard, her mind spinning with ideas.

I want to send the evil away just as you did, Sarah. But how? How did you do it?

Sarah Fear had died with that secret. But, Corky knew, the secret must live on in Sarah Fear's memory.

And Sarah Fear's memory was somewhere inside Corky's mind.

I just have to find it, Corky thought. I have to search until I find Sarah Fear's memory.

I have to let myself sink down, down, down into Sarah Fear's memory. And then maybe I can learn from Sarah Fear how to defeat this evil.

Corky suddenly realized that her entire body was trembling. Her hands and feet were ice cold. Her heart was thudding loudly in her chest.

As these wild ideas continued to whir through her mind, she returned to bed, lowered herself between the cool sheets, and pulled the covers up over her chin.

She closed her eyes and waited for her body to stop trembling, for the chills to stop, for her breathing to slow.

Then, with her eyes still closed, she tried to concentrate.

She pictured Sarah Fear. The swaying sailboat. The shimmering blue-gold water of the lake.

Forcing herself to breathe slowly, slowly . . . she sank into the evil spirit's mcmory.

Slipping into shadows darker than any she had ever experienced, she sank. Darker—and even darker. Such darkness, such depths inside her own mind.

Deeper. Until she heard low moans and soft whimpers. Cries of despair. And still deeper, into the ancient memory, into the memory of evil. The cries became howls. Anguished yelps of pain and suffering.

The darkness grew heavy and cold. Ghostly wisps of gray mist slithered like wounded animals in front of her. The howls of pain encircled her, pulled her down, down. . . .

As the anguished cries grew louder and the darkness became a living thing, a monstrous presence, a hungry, groping shadow that threatened to swallow her whole, Corky felt overwhelming fear.

As if all the fear from all the people inhabited by the evil spirit had poured into her.

Endless fear. Endless pain. All inside her own mind.

Crying out to her. Reaching for her. Trying to grab her and pull her down into untold horrors from centuries past.

No, I want to get out, Corky thought, struggling against the darkness, against the agony inside her. I don't want to be here. I don't want to hear this, to see this.

But she had no choice now. Now it was too late.

She was slipping back in time, deep into the memory of the foul thing inside her. . . .

Chapter 19

Sarah Fear's Secret

Standing at the rail, the sails rippling pleasantly beside her, Sarah Fear stared into the sparkling waters of Fear Lake.

The boat created gentle blue-green waves as it cut through the water. Sarah stared down at the water, sprinkled with the gold of reflected sunlight.

Such a calm day, she thought. So little wind. It will take forever to cross the lake.

That was okay with Sarah. She was in no hurry.

Sighing, she raised her pale face to the sun, closing her eyes. She stood still for a long time, letting the warmth settle over her.

"Aunt Sarah?" A young boy's voice interrupted her peace. "Come sit with Margaret and me."

Sarah opened her eyes and smiled down at Michael, her young nephew. Bathed in yellow sunlight, he

121

seemed to sparkle and shimmer like the water. His starched white sailor shirt and blond curls glowed in the bright light as if on fire. "Come sit with us."

"In a while," Sarah replied, placing a hand on his curls gently, reluctantly, as if they truly might be as hot as fire. "I'm enjoying the light breeze here. I feel like standing for a while."

"Where is Father?" Michael asked, searching the deck.

"He went below," Sarah replied, pointing to the stairs leading to the lower cabin. "He has a dreadful headache, poor man."

"We are moving too slowly," Michael complained.

"Yes—we want to go fast," his sister Margaret called from her seat across the wide deck.

Sarah laughed. "We can't go fast if there isn't any wind," she told them.

"Michael—would you like to take the wheel?" Jason Hardy called from behind them. Sarah turned, startled by his voice. She had almost forgotten he was on the boat.

Jason Hardy, Sarah's personal servant, was a tall, stern-faced man. His black mustache, waxed stiff, stuck out like bird wings on either side of his face. Dressed in a blue admiral's cap, matching blue blazer, and white sailor pants, he stood behind the wheel, motioning for Michael to join him.

"Me too!" cried Margaret, jumping up from her seat and starting toward the wheel.

"No, Margaret," Sarah scolded, laughing. "Piloting a sailboat is a man's job. That wouldn't be ladylike, would it?"

"I don't care." Margaret pouted, hands on her

waist. But she stopped obediently halfway across the deck.

Michael, beaming excitedly, grabbed the big wheel with both hands as Hardy instructed him on how to steer.

Sarah turned back to the rail, taking a deep breath. In the near distance she could see the green pines of Fear Island, the small round island in the center of the lake.

The children look so good, so healthy, she thought wistfully. It's the happiest I've seen them since their mother died.

Something fluttered near Sarah's face. Startled, she took a step back. It was a butterfly. Black and gold—a monarch butterfly.

You're a long way from shore, Sarah thought, admiring it as it hovered just over the rail. Did you follow us onto the sailboat this afternoon?

The butterfly fluttered silently just in front of her, hovering in place.

Such delicate beauty, Sarah thought. She reached out, wrapped her fingers around it, and crushed it.

A voice inside her head laughed. Cruelly.

It was a laugh Sarah had heard many times before.

"Aunt Sarah!" Margaret's surprised cry drowned out the sound. "What did you do to that butterfly?"

"Butterfly?" Sarah turned to face the little girl, a look of innocence on her face. "What butterfly, Margaret? I didn't see it."

She opened her palm and let the crushed remnants of the insect drop into the water. She wiped her hand on the rail.

One more murder, Sarah thought bitterly. One more . . .

A small cloud drifted across the sun. The rolling waters darkened around the boat.

How many more murders? Sarah wondered silently, squeezing the rail with both hands.

"Many more," came the reply. "As many as we desire," the familiar voice told her.

Sarah shuddered. "I want you gone," Sarah said aloud into the wind.

Laughter. "I will never leave you," said the voice, the voice of the evil that shared her body.

"I want you gone."

"I am part of you," the evil force declared.

"No!" Sarah protested.

"Aunt Sarah?" A hand tugged at her long skirt. "Aunt Sarah? Are you okay?"

"Yes . . . fine," Sarah answered quickly, turning to Margaret staring up at her, concern on her pretty, pale face. "I'm fine, Margaret."

Sarah turned to Jason Hardy. "Give Margaret a turn at the wheel. We won't tell anyone."

Margaret gave a squeal of joy and hurried to join her brother, her heavy black shoes loud on the wooden deck.

Sarah's hands wrapped tighter around the rail, and she leaned forward until she could feel cold spray on her face. So refreshing, so . . . clean.

She closed her eyes and remained still, her face catching the drops of spray. She loosened her grip on the rail and pressed hard against it with her corsetted waist.

I know how to kill you, she thought. I know how to get rid of you. I know how to free myself of your evil.

She waited for the voice inside her head to reply. She didn't have to wait long.

"You cannot kill me, Sarah."

A bitter smile formed on her pale lips. I know how.

And then a cold shudder of doubt made her grip the rail again.

I know how. I just don't know if I can bring myself to do it.

The evil laughter echoed once more in her mind. "I will move to the children," the evil spirit said. The cruelest threat of all.

"No!" Sarah screamed.

"Yes. I will live inside the children. First one, then the other. My evil shall live on, Sarah."

"No!"

She looked down at the mirrorlike surface. So clear, so pure.

And as she stared, visions of the deeds she had been forced to do seemed to float up to the surface. They were shadowy at first and murky, but as they floated nearer to the top, the pictures became bright and clear.

Sarah found herself facing her own evil.

She saw herself murdering the man at the mill, the man who had caused her husband's accident. She saw the expression of utter disbelief on the man's face as she grabbed him and shoved him from behind. And she heard the *crack* and *splat* as she pushed his head under the mill wheel. And his head was ground up as fine as the corn.

The woman who lived in the big house on the hill was even easier to murder. And what pleasure Sarah had taken in the crime. What delight. After all, the woman had insulted the Fears, insulted Simon Fear, insulted Sarah's dead husband, insulted the entire family.

She couldn't utter any insults with that length of clothesline wrapped around her neck. Sarah had pulled the clothesline tighter and tighter, until the woman's face was bright purple, as purple as the violets in her garden. So tight that the rope actually disappeared under the woman's skin. And the blood had flowed out in a perfect ring.

The tiny town of Shadyside was in an uproar now. Who could be doing these ghastly murders?

They were all frightened of the Fear family. But they sent the young police constable anyway. He was so young and handsome, Sarah thought. And he asked so many questions.

Too many questions.

How lucky that Sarah was boiling up an enormous pot of potatoes when the young police officer arrived. She had only to shove his head deep into the boiling water, and wait.

What a struggle he'd put up. Thrashing his arms.

But Sarah had held his head under until the thrashing stopped. Until his breathing stopped, until he was dead, and he slumped lifeless over the black cast-iron stove.

All of his hair had floated off, floated to the top of the pot. And when she finally pulled him up, his head was as white as a boiled potato and nearly as soft.

So much for the police investigation.

The residents of the town grew quiet and fearful. Neighbor avoided neighbor. Rumors were whispered, but few words of accusation were murmured aloud.

These pictures surfaced in the mirrorlike lake water as Sarah leaned over the rail and stared down.

"No more," she whispered aloud.

"There will be more," the evil spirit inside her promised. "There will be many more."

"No more," Sarah repeated, shaking her head.

I know how to kill you, she thought, taking a deep breath.

I know how to get rid of you.

"I will move to the children," came the ugly threat once again. "I will live inside Michael. I will live inside Margaret."

No, you won't, Sarah argued.

No. You will die, evil spirit.

I know how to drown you.

The cruel laughter rang in her head. "Fool. I cannot be drowned."

Yes, you can, Sarah told it, a bitter smile spreading on her pretty face. Yes, you can. You can drown. You can.

"I cannot be drowned."

You can be drowned, Sarah told it silently, if *I* drown first.

"No," the voice inside her quickly replied, but doubt and surprise colored the single word for the first time.

If I kill myself with you inside, Sarah told it, then you will die with me.

Sarah turned back to the children. Jason Hardy stood between them as they enthusiastically guided the wheel together.

So innocent, she thought.

They don't know anything at all about their evil aunt Sarah. And I hope they never will.

Sarah had known for a long time how to rid herself, how to rid the world, of the ancient evil force. She had known that she had to die in order for it to be killed.

But ending her own life was too frightening to think about. Too frightening to imagine—until the evil spirit mentioned the children.

I have to save them, Sarah thought. I have to save them *now*.

Her throat constricted as she stared down into the water. She uttered a low cry and leaned forward a little farther.

And as she leaned, the boat tilted, reared up as if facing a strong wind.

Sarah was tossed back. She landed sharply against the mast and toppled to the deck in a sitting position. She struggled to get back up as the craft began to twirl.

"What's happening?" She heard Margaret's frightened voice behind her. "Why are we spinning?"

"It isn't windy!"

"What's wrong with the boat?"

Sarah knew what was wrong with the boat. The evil spirit was working hard to keep her from throwing herself over the rail into the water.

Around and around, like a carousel, the boat spun. Picking up speed, it sent up a high wall of water around it.

Dizzy and terrified, her heart thudding, Sarah reached for the mast. She grabbed it to pull herself up.

The boat reared up violently then, and dipped low into the tossing water. Sarah's hand slipped off the mast, and she fell hard to the deck once again.

The sky was black now, as black as night.

The ring of water tossed up by the spinning boat encircled the boat and threatened to roll over it.

"You cannot drown me!" the evil voice screamed inside Sarah's head. "My evil lives forever!"

As the boat spun faster and faster, Sarah heard the terrified cries of her little niece and nephew.

"You will not get to them," she said out loud through gritted teeth. This time she pulled herself to her feet.

Water crashed down heavily and washed over the deck like a tidal wave. The boat heaved as it twirled, and the waters tossed up high, frothing eerily in a circle around it.

"You will not get the children!" Sarah Fear declared, shouting at the evil inside her.

She shut her eyes tightly and lunged blindly to the rail.

"Aunt Sarah!" She heard the children's shrill voices, distant now, as if miles away. "Aunt Sarah! Come back!"

"You cannot drown me!"

But I must!

"You haven't the courage to drown yourself!"

Was the ancient evil right?

Did she have the courage?

Could she sacrifice her life, her young life, for Michael and Margaret?

"There will be more evil to come, Sarah. There will be much more evil."

"Noooooooo!"

And Sarah Fear dived under the rail. Into the dark, tossing waters under the black sky.

Down into the cold water. Churning and bubbling.

Down she plunged, gulping in water.

Inhaling the heavy water.

Taking in mouthfuls as she descended, her hair loose and floating gracefully above her head like a kind of sea creature, her arms pulling her deeper into the darkness.

Her lungs filling with the heavy water.

Choking. Sputtering.

No longer breathing.

No longer seeing.

I'm drowning, she thought. I'm not breathing now. Soon I will be gone. Soon, I hope.

And as Sarah drowned, the evil thrashed inside her, fighting desperately. As the water invaded her lungs, the spirit struggled to free itself.

She felt it try to thrust itself out from her throat. The water bubbled as a stream of green gas erupted from her mouth.

The eruption was so powerful that it forced Sarah to the surface. She saw the sailboat overturned, upside down.

The children, she thought.

And then she was underwater again.

The water was hot. Boiling. Scalding hot.

Burning her skin. So unbearably hot.

And the green gas poured into the tossing, boiling water.

"Up. Rise up," the voice told her. *"Rise up and save us both!"*

But Sarah plunged lower, forcing herself down.

Now she could feel two fears at once. Her own and that of the ancient spirit.

Both frightened now. Both about to die.

Both dying.

Both.

The boiling, bubbling water churned around her. The flowing green gas encircled her, shutting out all light. The spirit was trapped in Sarah's drowning body.

The evil voice cried out. "NOOOOOOOOOOO!"

A wail of rage, of disbelief.

The cry was strong at first. Then weak. Then a whimper of faint protest. The green gas bubbled away.

Sarah Fear's eyes were bulging wide. But she saw nothing now.

Not even the still, still blackness.

For she—and the evil—were dead.

Then—more darkness. Rapidly swirling darkness. Black moving against black.

Corky slept without moving, as if in a coma, her breathing slow and silent.

Deeper, she sank. Deeper into old memories.

Shadows formed, twisting and bending in the darkness.

Deeper.

Deeper.

No longer in Sarah Fear's memory.

Sinking deeper inside the mind of the ancient evil.

Deeper.

Until she entered the memory of the evil spirit itself.

Now Corky looked out through the evil spirit's eyes.

And stared in bitter horror at the velvet-lined walls of a coffin.

She was inside the coffin. Six feet under the ground. Trapped inside. Hunkered low against the closed lid.

Inside the rotting corpse of Sarah Fear.

Yes. Sarah Fear was dead. Drowned in Fear Lake. And up above, poking up through the loamy cemetery ground, stood Sarah's gravestone.

Surrounded by four other stones. Stones for Michael, for Margaret, for their father, and for Jason Hardy. All dead. All drowned in the boiling waters of the lake.

And now the evil spirit shared Sarah's grave. Imprisoned beside the foul, decaying body it once possessed.

Defeated by Sarah's courage. Trapped by Sarah's final sacrifice.

It waited.

Waited eagerly for a live body to come along and free it.

Waited. Waited.

Staring at the worms that invaded Sarah's grinning skull.

* * *

Corky woke.

She sat up, alert, wide awake. Trembling. Her sheets were tangled, hot, and damp from perspiration.

She could still see Sarah Fear's corpse, the decaying walls of the small coffin. She could still hear the roar of the churning lake in her mind, still hear the hiss of the escaping green gas, still hear the hideous howl of the evil spirit dying.

Corky swallowed hard. She realized she was crying. Hot tears rolled down her even hotter cheeks. Sarah Fear has told me all I need to know, she thought, letting the tears fall.

To kill the evil, I have to kill . . . myself.

PART THREE

Hot Water

Chapter 20

Kimmy Must Die

Corky drifted back into a troubled sleep. When she awoke again, sunlight was streaming in through her bedroom windows, the curtains fluttering in a soft breeze.

She sat up, stretching, and stared down at the foot of her bed into the bulging eyes of a hideous orange-fleshed face covered with stitched-up scars.

Corky opened her mouth to scream. But then recognized the intruder as Sean's rubber mask from Halloween.

Sean must have placed it on the bedpost while she slept.

"Way to go, Sean," she said out loud, shaking her head. Reaching over, she pulled the disgusting mask off its perch and tossed it into the corner.

My little brother is a real monster, she thought.

137

As she lowered her feet to the floor and stretched again, the images of her dream, the images from Sarah Fear's memory, came back, forced themselves vividly into her mind, as vividly as if she had lived them herself.

But how can I kill myself? she asked herself, staring at the rubber mask she had tossed to the floor.

Never see Sean again? Never see my parents again? Never go out? Never fall in love? Never get married? Have a family? Have a *life?*

I'm only sixteen, Corky thought miserably. Sixteen. Too young to die.

"No!" she declared aloud. "No way!"

She thought of Bobbi. Poor Bobbi—she never lived long enough to . . . to *do anything!*

I owe it to Bobbi, Corky thought, standing up unsteadily, her mind racing. I owe it to my poor dead sister to go on living. To have a full life—a full, happy life.

But how?

She could sense the evil stirring inside her. Waking, it started to dull her thoughts and she began to fade into the background.

She began to drift away—inside her own body.

I'm going to ignore it, Corky decided.

That's how I'll deal with it. I'll ignore it, and it'll go away.

If it tries to do something terrible, I can deal with it. I know I can. I just won't cooperate.

If I ignore it. Or if I fight it. I mean, I'll ignore it. And then . . .

138

She knew she wasn't thinking clearly. But how could she? Her room was so far away . . . the windows so tiny and distant . . . the light so dim.

"No!" she cried, struggling to resist the force taking over her mind. "No! I'm ignoring you!"

She heard cruel laughter. Then her bedroom walls began to quake.

"No!"

The flowers—the red carnations, the blue gardenias —all the flowers on the wallpaper started to spin.

"No!"

The flowers spun wildly, then flew off the wallpaper, spinning up to the ceiling.

"No! Please—no!"

Corky heard the laughter again, loud laughter inside her head as the red and blue flowers rained down on her. Another peal of cruel laughter.

Turning away from the wall, Corky quickly pulled on a pair of gray sweat pants and a wrinkled blue T-shirt. Then, she ran out onto the landing and started down the stairs. But as she stepped onto the first one, a row of razor blades popped up from the carpet.

"Ow!" She cried out as her bare foot nearly missed getting sliced.

Leaning on the banister, she stared down as razor blades popped up with a loud snap on each step.

She flung herself onto the banister and slid down on her stomach. The banister was burning hot by the time she leapt off at the bottom.

"Corky—what on earth?!" her mother exclaimed.

She was standing in the hallway, a bundle of dirty clothes in her arms.

"Oh. Sorry, Mom," Corky said, swallowing hard. She looked up at the stairs. The razor blades were gone.

"You slept so late," Mrs. Corcoran said, dropping the clothing by the basement steps. "It's almost noon."

Corky opened her mouth to speak. But what could she say? No words came out. She followed her mother into the kitchen.

"I'm going to fry up a couple of eggs for you," Corky's mom said, gazing fretfully at her daughter. "You look hungry."

"Yes," Corky said weakly. She hoped her mother didn't see how hard she was breathing, how her entire body was trembling. Trying to steady herself, to appear calm, Corky climbed onto a stool at the kitchen counter and watched as Mrs. Corcoran made two eggs.

"Toast? Juice?" her mother asked.

"I guess," Corky replied, struggling to keep her voice low and steady, struggling against the wild, swirling thoughts in her head.

Her mother stared at her, as if examining her. "You feeling okay, Corky?"

"No, Mom. I'm inhabited by an evil spirit. It's inside me, controlling me, and I can't do anything about it."

"Very funny," Mrs. Corcoran said sarcastically, rolling her eyes. She tapped her metal spatula beside the frying pan. "Do all teenagers develop such

140

gross senses of humor, or is it just a specialty of yours?"

I'm telling the truth, Mom! But you don't want to hear it, *do* you? You don't want to believe it.

"Where is Sean?" Corky asked. The words weren't hers. The evil spirit was forcing her to change the subject.

"He and your dad are at his baseball game," Mrs. Corcoran replied. She scraped the eggs from the pan. "You haven't spent much time with your brother lately."

"He left me a little reminder of himself this morning," Corky said, picturing the gruesome rubber mask.

Her mother deposited the two fried eggs on a plate and set it down in front of Corky. "Get your toast when it's ready," she said, and disappeared to deal with the laundry.

Corky stared down at the eggs, then reluctantly picked up her fork.

As she gazed at the plate, the eggs shimmered, then transformed themselves. Corky's mouth dropped open as she now stared at two enormous wet eyeballs.

"No!"

The eyeballs stared back at her. Their color darkened to gray. Then the gray became a sickening green, the green of decay, and a foul odor rose up from the plate. As the putrid aroma filled the air and the eyeballs shriveled and wrinkled, Corky gagged and leapt off the stool.

The laughter, the cruel, cold laughter, followed her as she ran blindly back up to her room.

I give up, she thought, flinging herself facedown on her bed. She started to sob, but her breath caught in her throat. A wave of nausea swept over her as she felt the evil force move within her.

The phone rang. It took her a while to recognize the sound. It rang again. Again.

"Hello?"

"Hello, Corky? It's me." Kimmy.

"Hi, Kimmy. How's it going?" She tried to sound casual, but her voice broke.

"Okay. I was just worried about you," Kimmy replied. "I haven't seen you since—since camp. And you were so sick and everything. I mean, it was just such a *disaster*. Are you better? I mean, are you okay?"

Why is Kimmy calling? Corky asked herself bitterly. She isn't my friend, she thought, her features tightening in an unpleasant expression of hatred. Kimmy has never been my friend. She tried to kill me once. Tried to drown me.

"I saw Hannah yesterday, and she said she hadn't seen you either," Kimmy continued brightly. "So Hannah and I were just wondering—"

Don't worry, Corky thought coldly. I'll be seeing Hannah soon. Very soon. And when I see her, Hannah won't be happy to see *me*.

"I'm feeling better," Corky told Kimmy.

"Oh, good!" Kimmy exclaimed. "I really was worried about you. I mean, after all that went down. You know."

Yes, I *do* know, Corky thought angrily. I *do* know what you're talking about, Kimmy.

And I do know that you know too much.

You have to die, Corky decided. You have to die now, Kimmy.

"Hey, Kimmy, are you doing anything this afternoon?" Corky asked, winding the phone cord around her wrist.

"No, not really," Kimmy replied. "Why? You want to hang out or something?"

"Yeah," Corky answered quickly. "I really want to talk to you."

"Great!" Kimmy exclaimed. "I want to talk to you too."

"Can you meet me up on River Ridge in about half an hour?" Corky asked. River Ridge was a high cliff overlooking the Cononka River.

"River Ridge?" Kimmy sounded surprised. "Sure, I guess. See you in half an hour."

Corky untwisted the cord from her arm and replaced the receiver.

Kimmy must die in water, she decided, picturing the high cliff and the river flowing beneath it.

Kimmy must die the way Sarah Fear died.

The way my sister Bobbi died.

Now.

143

Chapter 21

Kimmy Dies

Dark storm clouds filtered out the sun, casting a wash of eerie yellow over the afternoon sky. The air was heavy and wet . . . and very still. There was no wind.

Corky left her car at the end of the road and walked across the hard ground to the cliff edge. Behind her, the silent woods darkened as the black clouds hovered lower.

There was no one else around.

Standing on the rocky ledge that jutted out over the steep drop, Corky stared down at the wide brown river below. The Conononka, she saw, was high on its banks, flowing rapidly, a steady rush of sound rising up the cliff.

Ever since moving to Shadyside, Corky had enjoyed coming up to River Ridge. It was the highest spot around. Beyond the river she could see the town stretched out like some kind of model or miniature. To the north, the woods formed a winding, dark ribbon on the horizon.

It's so peaceful up here, Corky thought. Even though she could still see Shadyside, she felt far away from it. As if she were floating over the town in a tranquil world of her own.

Corky took a step back and glanced at her watch. Where was Kimmy?

Let's get this show on the road, she thought impatiently. She gazed up at the darkening sky, the black clouds so low now over her head. It's so humid, she thought. The air is so still and sticky.

She realized she was perspiring, her T-shirt clinging to her back. The back of her neck started to itch.

Come *on,* Kimmy. Don't you want to see the surprise I have for you?

I'm going to give Kimmy a flying lesson, she thought, her lips forming a cruel smile.

A flying lesson. And then a *drowning* lesson.

Hearing a car door slam behind her, Corky turned. Kimmy, dressed in a cropped red shirt over blue Lycra bike shorts, walked quickly toward her. Kimmy's car was parked next to hers at the end of the road.

"Think it's okay to park here?" Kimmy called.

"Sure," Corky answered. "There's no one else around." And you won't need it to leave, Corky added to herself.

Kimmy's round cheeks were bright pink; her crimped black hair was damp and disheveled. "I thought it would be cooler up here," she complained, brushing a strand of hair from over her eyes.

You'll be cooler in a moment, Corky thought. "There's no wind at all today," Corky said. "Look at the trees."

They both turned to gaze back at the woods. "Not a leaf moving," Kimmy said, and focused on Corky, a questioning expression on her face. "What are we *doing* up here?"

Corky chuckled. "I don't know. I thought it'd be a nice place to talk. You know."

Kimmy glanced up at the rain-heavy clouds. "We're going to get drenched."

"That would feel good," Corky said, and took a step toward the cliff's edge. Kimmy followed her.

"You're feeling better?" Kimmy asked with genuine concern.

Corky nodded. "Yeah. A lot." And I'm going to feel even better in a few seconds, Corky thought to herself.

"That was so terrible at camp," Kimmy said. "I mean, you getting sick like that. What a disaster."

"Yeah . . . what a disaster," Corky repeated with a grim smile.

"And all that stupid stuff with Hannah," Kimmy added, avoiding Corky's eyes. "You know I didn't do any of that stuff to her. You believe me, don't you?"

"Yes, of course," Corky replied. "I didn't do it either."

"So . . . what do you think?" Kimmy asked, turning to face Corky, searching her face. "I mean, what do you think happened?"

"I think Hannah did those things to herself," Corky told her, forcing herself to keep a straight face.

"The scalding bath? The braid?"

"I think she faked the scalding bath," Corky said in a low voice. "I think she just screamed and carried on. I don't think she was really burned—just a little red."

"And you think she cut her own hair?" Kimmy asked.

Corky nodded solemnly.

"But *why?*" Kimmy asked shrilly.

"To get both of us in trouble," Corky said. "To make us look bad. To get us kicked off the squad so she could be the star."

"Wow!" Kimmy's mouth dropped open in dismay. "I never thought of that. Never. It never occurred to me that Hannah . . ." Her voice trailed off as she thought about it.

"Well, what *did* you think?" Corky asked sharply. "That I did it? Did you suspect me, Kimmy?"

"No!" Kimmy protested, her cheeks reddening. "No, I didn't, Corky. I—I didn't know *what* to think. I knew the evil spirit had to be around. I knew the evil had to be responsible. But I didn't know where. I mean, I didn't know *who*. I just . . ."

Corky felt a drop of rain on her forehead. Enough stalling around, she thought. I'd better get this over with.

"The evil is around," Corky said, lowering her voice to a whisper. She felt another large raindrop, this time on top of her head. Then one on her shoulder.

"Huh?" Again Kimmy's mouth dropped open in

surprise. "You mean—Hannah? Do you think it's inside Hannah?"

"Maybe," Corky replied mysteriously.

"It's starting to rain," Kimmy said, holding out her palms. "Maybe we should go back to your car and talk."

"Okay," Corky replied. "But first look down there." She pointed straight down over the cliff's edge. "I've been trying to figure out what that is, but I can't."

"What?" Kimmy leaned over and peered down at the rushing river.

Corky reached out and shoved Kimmy. Hard.

Kimmy uttered a loud shriek as she went over the side. Her arms thrashed wildly as she dropped head-first.

A grin spread over Corky's face as she stood, hands on hips, and watched Kimmy plunge to her death.

Chapter 22

Triumph of Evil

"**K**immy is dead."

Corky said the words out loud, a triumphant smile spreading across her face.

Raindrops fell gently, a few at a time. Standing on the cliff edge, Corky peered down at the brown, flowing river water.

"Kimmy is dead."

Still smiling, Corky started to leave. But from somewhere deep inside her a muffled voice shouted: "No!"

She hesitated.

I have to leave now. Kimmy is dead. Now I have to take care of Debra.

And again the distant, muffled voice cried out: "No!"

The smile faded on Corky's face, and her eyes narrowed unpleasantly.

149

"No!"

The rain fell harder. The gentle *ping* on the ground became a steady drumroll. I have to finish Debra now.

"No!"

The protesting voice was Corky's. The real Corky trying to make herself heard, struggling to regain control.

"No! I can't let this happen!" The real Corky's voice grew stronger.

"I am in control now!" the evil force cried out. *"Stay back! I'm warning you!"*

"No!" Corky called out with renewed strength.

"No!" From somewhere deep in her own mind Corky lashed out, pushed her way forward, pressed against the heavy evil.

The horror of Kimmy's death—the horror of what Corky had just done—had reached through the evil, had brought Corky to life. She knew she had no choice. She had to fight it. Now.

"Stay back!" the ancient evil warned. *"Stay back where you belong!"*

"No!" Corky fought back, struggling within herself, struggling blindly as the ground disappeared, along with the sky, the trees, everything.

She was nowhere. In a gray limbo. Fighting a foe she couldn't see . . . fighting herself.

"I have to die!" she told herself. "I have to die now!"

And another part of her said, "No. I cannot die! I am too young. I want to *live!*"

"Die—and force this evil to die with you!"

"No—I can't die! I'm too afraid! I want to live!"

"You cannot live with this ghastly thing inside you! You must die to save your friends, your family!"

"Get back!" growled the evil inside her head. *"Get back now!"*

"No!" Corky cried.

"Kimmy!" she screamed. "Kimmy—I'm so sorry!"

I am evil, Corky told herself. I am evil, and I must die!

"I must live!" the evil force declared. *"Get back or suffer a thousand deaths inside your own body!"*

"Nooooo!"

With a final scream Corky spun around—and stepped to the cliff's edge.

She stopped to peer down, her chest heaving, her blood pulsing against her temples.

No! I can't do it!

"I can't!" she screamed. "I'm too young! I can't!"

She felt the evil stir, rising up heavily, triumphantly, inside her. "I can't! I can't!"

She took a step back.

Defeated.

"I can't die! I won't die!"

"Others will die," the evil spirit said inside her. *"We will live forever!"*

Chapter 23

Into the Water

"Let us go," the evil said. *"We have work to do."*

Corky obediently took another step back.

Then suddenly, impulsively, courageously, she stopped. Raising both fists to the dark sky, she shut her eyes and uttered a howl of anguish.

And plunged off the cliff.

The fall was like a dream.

Was that *her* screaming all the way down?

She hit the water hard and instantly sank into the murky brown depths.

"I must live!" the evil protested.

But Corky dived toward the river bottom. The strong current swept her along. Down, down, down.

She started to choke. The thick muddy water poured into her open mouth. She tasted the grit, the sourness of it.

I'm choking. I'm going to die.

But I don't *want* to die.

I want to live!

I can't drown. I *can't* die!

I have to live! I *have* to!

But I can't. I have no choice.

I have made my choice.

To die!

She gasped in another mouthful of the thick, disgusting water.

And choked violently as she thrashed helplessly under the dark waters.

As she choked, the evil began to erupt from her mouth.

She thrashed blindly as the force flowed out of her, blasting the water, churning it, heating it with its evil.

Hotter.

The water grew hotter as Corky thrashed and choked.

Hotter.

Until the river boiled.

And still the evil poured out.

The evil flowed into the churning brown waters, protesting its fate, a howl of fury rising in Corky's ears, raging through the tossing waters.

Hotter.

The brown water bubbled and boiled up. Tall geysers erupted toward the black sky. Even hotter.

Corky writhed in pain as the water scalded her struggling body.

I'm dying—dying. . . .

She felt suddenly light. The evil had departed.

And then heavier again. Heavy with the thick water that choked her, filling her lungs. *"I'm drowning!"*

She heard the evil spirit's startled cry. *"I'm drowning!"*

And then Corky drowned. She felt as if she were shrinking.

Shrinking until she was nothing but a tiny acorn floating in the water. Then a dot. A lifeless dot. She knew the evil spirit had shrunk too.

And knowing this, she died.

Chapter 24

Another Death

Raindrops pelted the tumultuous tossing waters. Steam rose up from the boiling surface, forming an eerie white ceiling of fog over the river.

Corky's body floated to the top, bobbing like a small rubber raft.

Watching from the depths, the evil spirit uttered its own death cry, an unending wail of despair.

Its power boiled the water, pushed the river over its banks, sent high waves crashing against the cliff beside it.

The thunder of the crashing waves drowned out the thunder in the sky. The anguished howl of the ancient evil weakened and began to fade. The waters still bubbled and steamed.

"You can't die!" the spirit wailed, tossing Corky's body over the surface.

"You cannot die. You cannot betray me! I am you, and you are me! You cannot die!"

Weaker.

The waters began to cool. The eerie white steam drifted apart in the heavy rain.

Weaker.

"I won't let you die!" the ancient force declared. Gathering its strength, it pushed the waters beneath Corky, pushed her up, up—until she rose above the water, suspended in the white mist.

"I won't let you die! You are free now! You are out of the water! You are free!"

Hovering over the water like a sagging helium balloon, Corky's body slumped lifelessly, her head back, her eyes staring blindly up at the storm clouds.

"NOOOOOOOOOOOOOOOO!" The evil spirit's wail of defeat rose like a siren, then faded to silence.

Corky's body dropped back into the water without making a splash.

"You are dead," the spirit admitted. "And in dying, you have killed me."

Now the thunder in the sky roared louder than the crash of the ebbing waves. In that crash, the spirit was thrown from her body.

The river flowed quietly again.

The water quickly cooled.

The evil faded, then disappeared. Washed away forever in the rain-stirred brown river current.

Chapter 25

A Smile

Kimmy had hit the water hard, on her stomach, and then plunged to the bottom. Paralyzed from shock, she could do nothing but let the current move her.

But the cold water quickly revived her. Raising both arms and kicking off from the soft river floor, she forced her way to the surface—in time to see Corky's dive.

Sheets of rain blinded Kimmy as she struggled against the current to get to her friend.

The tossing waves pushed her back.

The water heated up, boiled, and swirled.

What's going on? Kimmy wondered, ducking under the waves, stroking desperately, her feet kicking the hot, frothy water.

What is *happening?*

I can't get to you, Corky.

I can't get there.

Please be okay. Please. Please. Please.

Please.

The word became an endless chant in her mind. The sky darkened as the torrents of rain pelted down. Kimmy searched in vain for Corky.

And then—to her amazement, to her horror—she thought she saw Corky rise up from the water.

Squinting through the rain, pulling against the current, Kimmy stared at the figure hovering in the white mist, floating over the surface of the water, suspended in the air.

"Corky!"

Kimmy swallowed a mouthful of the hot brown water.

Choking and sputtering, she struggled to breathe.

When she looked back up, Corky was gone. Had she slipped back into the water?

Or had she been some kind of mirage, merely Kimmy's imagination? "Corky! I can't get to you! Where are you? Where are you?"

Be okay. Please. Please. Please. Please.

An object floated on the surface, bobbing on the waves, carried by the strong current.

Kimmy shrieked as she recognized Corky's lifeless form.

Gasping for each breath, her arms aching, her chest about to explode, Kimmy swam frantically toward Corky's body. Remembering her lifesaving course, Kimmy grabbed Corky in a cross-chest carry and paddled desperately against the current.

Dead. Dead. Corky is dead.

Kimmy pulled Corky onto the grassy shore, then stood up unsteadily. Her legs trembled as she gasped, sucking in air, not noticing the cold rain beating down on her.

When she knew her heart wasn't going to explode, Kimmy dropped to her knees, rolled Corky onto her stomach, leaned over her lifeless body, crying, sobbing, trembling.

She pushed down with all her weight on Corky's back. Then released.

Then pushed again, sobbing as she worked.

Pushed and released.

Nothing. No sign of life.

Pushed and released.

Pushed and released.

Until a convulsion of brown water spewed from Corky's lifeless mouth.

Pushed and released.

Kimmy sobbed as she worked, salty tears mixing with cool raindrops on her feverish cheeks.

Pushed and released.

Corky's body rose with another convulsion. Another thick gob of river water rushed out of her mouth. She's dead, Kimmy knew. Corky's dead.

But she pushed anyway, leaning forward, shivering from the cold, from the wet as she worked, sobbing.

Corky's dead.

I'm not doing any good. I have to stop.

I have to stop. I have to get home. I have to tell someone.

Pushed and released. Pushed and released. Even though it was too late.

Corky groaned as the murky water poured out of her mouth.

She stirred. Coughed. Opened her eyes.

And saw only dirt. Tall grass. Her face was down in the dirt, her eyes covered with a film of water.

She blinked. Choked. Putrid brown water spilled over her chin.

"Corky! Corky!"

Where was the voice coming from?

Corky raised her head. She turned to see a girl on her knees beside her.

"Kimmy!"

Kimmy smiled down at her. "You're alive!"

"Kimmy—you're okay!"

Kimmy tried to reply, but tears choked her words.

Corky coughed. Her mouth tasted sour. She reached up to brush the matted hair off her forehead. The rain pounded down around them, over them. Neither girl seemed to notice.

"I'm so cold," Corky finally said, shuddering.

Kimmy helped her to sit up. "I thought you were dead," Kimmy said, shivering too.

Corky didn't seem to hear her. She sat up and gazed wide-eyed around her, ignoring the rain. After a long while she climbed unsteadily to her feet. "Let's go."

"I'll help you." Kimmy wrapped an arm around Corky's trembling shoulders.

"I'm alive," Corky said, still dazed. "I'm alive and you're alive."

"Yes," Kimmy said, and smiled. Slowly she started to lead Corky up the trail to the top of the cliff.

"Oh!" Corky uttered a frightened cry and pointed back at the water. "Look."

Corky turned from her friend, back to the dark waters. Something stirred near the shore. She took a reluctant step closer, squinting against the rain.

A light spot in the water. A circle of light.

And inside it, a reflection.

A face.

Corky stared hard, trembling, breathing hard.

It's Bobbi's face, she realized.

It's Bobbi's face in the water.

It's Bobbi.

And she's smiling.

Corky stared, smiling back, until the reflection broke into tiny pinpoints of light. Bobbi's smiling face dimmed and then shimmered away.

Feeling peaceful, Corky turned back to Kimmy. "Let's go home."

Arm in arm they began to make their way up the cliff through the cool, cleansing rain.

Epilogue

"Tigers, let's score!
Six points and more!
Tigers, let's score!
Six points and more!"

The cheers rang out through the gym. Corky had done this chant a million times. But now it seemed fresh and new.

"That sounds great!" Miss Green exclaimed from the sidelines.

Even *she* notices the difference, Corky thought.

She flashed Kimmy a smile as the girls got into position for the pyramid. "Don't drop me," Corky teased.

"Who—me?" Kimmy replied with exaggerated innocence.

Corky made her way to the top.

"Liberties! In rhythm!" Miss Green called, gripping the whistle around her neck.

The six cheerleaders obediently struck the well-practiced pose.

"Excellent!" Miss Green said. "Straighten your back, Ronnie."

Time for my jump, thought Corky. She glanced down at Kimmy.

Her throat tightened. A moment of panic.

Then she stepped off.

Kimmy caught her easily.

"Perfect!" Miss Green declared.

The girls all cheered.

"Way to go!" Hannah slapped Corky on the back.

"Are you putting on weight?" Kimmy teased.

After practice Corky, Kimmy, Ronnie, and Debra squeezed into a booth at The Corner, all four of them talking at once. One of the basketball players had told Ronnie a dirty joke she couldn't wait to share. Corky laughed hard at Ronnie's joke even though she'd heard it before. Debra had news about Gary Brandt's new girlfriend. Kimmy wanted to discuss how she should have her hair cut on Saturday.

The waitress stood impatiently, tapping her pencil against her pad, waiting for the four friends to stop talking so she could take their order.

"I'll just have a Coke," Debra said finally.

"Me too," Kimmy said. "A Coke and an order of fries."

The waitress turned her attention to Corky.

"Know what I have a craving for?" Corky asked Kimmy, peering at her over the top of the menu.

Kimmy shrugged. "No. What?"

"Pea soup," Corky said softly.

"No way!" her three companions shouted in unison.

"I'll have a burger and fries," Corky told the waitress.

All four girls collapsed in riotous laughter.

The waitress headed back to the kitchen, shaking her head, wondering what on earth could be funny about pea soup. . . .

About the Author

R. L. STINE doesn't know *where* he gets the ideas for his scary books! But he wants to assure worried readers that none of the horrors of FEAR STREET ever happened to him in real life.

Bob lives in New York City with his wife and twelve-year-old son. He is the author of more than two dozen bestselling mysteries and thrillers for Young Adult readers. He also writes scary novels for younger readers.

In addition to his publishing work, he is Head Writer of the children's TV show "Eureeka's Castle," seen on Nickelodeon.

THE NIGHTMARES
NEVER END. . .
WHEN YOU VISIT

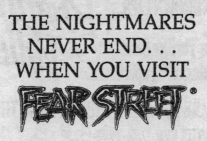

Next . . .
THE BEST FRIEND
(Coming December 1992)

Becka Norwood is completely confused when Honey Perkins moves next door and tells everyone at Shadyside High that the two girls used to be best friends. Becka doesn't remember Honey at all!

And now Honey is set on becoming Becka's best friend again . . . no matter what it takes. Honey moves in on Becka's life—and then the horrible accidents begin.

As Christmas approaches, Becka becomes alarmed. Does Honey just want a friend? Or does she want *much more?*